The Canary

Jacqueline T. Moore

Cover Art:
Michelle Crocker

http://mlcdesigns4you.weebly.com/

Publisher's Note:

This is a work of fiction. All names, characters, places, and events are the work of the author's imagination.

Any resemblance to real persons, places, or events is coincidental.

Solstice Publishing - www.solsticepublishing.com

For Ruthann !

THE CANARY

Jacqueline T. Moore

Jacqueline T. Moore

2014

Dedication

For my mother, Myra Lee Turner, who wore the yellow diamond all of my life, and for my daughter, Julie Anne Jacobs, who will wear it after me. I love you.

Chapter 1

MYRA

Myra almost made it to 'I do'. Almost.

"Sorry Jesus." She gagged. There was an offering basket close by that saved the pastor's robe from wearing her breakfast. Her mama held her hair, her papa held her shoulders, and her man held his breath.

"My God, that girl got in the family way fast," whispered Everett to himself as he stood on one side of his bride, while Myra's father stood on the other, facing the Methodist minister. Mr. Everett Gallaway was ten years Myra's senior, and had gone to school. He was so very handsome with his jet hair greased back. Myra thought if she had to settle, he'd do. Besides, you couldn't argue with a swelling belly. Not at her tender age of just turned thirteen.

"I do."

As soon as Junior was born, the young family took the long journey from Charleston to Galveston with a promise of a steady job for Everett. By 1889 the reconstruction increased rail travel seven fold. They were met at end of their trip by Myra's aunt and uncle, her father's brother, Harry Dickenson, and his wife Ada.

"Oh my darlings..." Aunt Ada bustled around them as they stood on the platform, waiting for the porter to bring their trunks. "Let me look at you. Give me that baby. You must be exhausted." Myra nodded. "Precious, you look just like your grandfather," Ada cooed to the baby. "Harry, look at this child. Isn't he just the spittin' image of your brother?"

"He's spittin' all right. Hand me that diaper." Uncle Harry grinned and took the cloth from an overwhelmed Myra. "You don't need worry about a thing, Niece. You are home now." He gave the burp mop to his wife, kissed Myra's cheek, and shook Everett's hand.

They stayed with Aunt Ada and Uncle Harry until the young father's first pay. Thanks to Uncle Harry's connections, Everett got a job at one of the counting houses on the wharves. There he was among many men who recorded the import and export of goods that the giant sailing ships carried. They worked six day a week, off only for the Sabbath.

Daddy's dowry rented them a three-room furnished shotgun. They put Junior in the kitchen by the stove to keep him warm and besides, way in the back they didn't hear him holler so much. Myra lost number two there. Later on they got a bungalow where she had the rest. Uncle Harry called it 'The Shoe', what with all five children.

You wouldn't think that Myra's next babies, Benjamin and Frank, were twins since they were so dissimilar. They even had different colored hair. Myra always felt that the way she carried them made some difference, but she had no words for the hair. Benjy met his mama first, all fat and attitude, with his black hair slicked back just like his daddy's. His cry was strong and Myra thought she was done. When Franky came instead of placenta, the entire room was shocked, including Dr. McKnight. He knew she was big, but damn…two? He was as surprised as anyone. This child looked like a wet cat, all scrawny and blue, with the littlest bit of red fuzz on his head. His cries were squawks, not squalls, and Myra instantly loved her least'n more than life itself.

She would feed them both at the same time, but made sure Franky got the fuller breast. He was not strong enough to suckle hard and the feedings took longer than his brother. Every once in a while Junior would toddle over for his share and he learned quickly to stand by the bigger baby to wait his turn. When Benjy was done, Junior would get a snack and a hug. Franky seemed unaware of the brother switch and just kept right on nursing. Everett thought his milky mate was out of her mind, not using baby bottles and cow's milk, but didn't say anything. He knew that what happened in The Shoe was Myra's business and what happened in the counting house was his.

Old wives said nursing stops new babies. Theophilis and Nora Lee came in the next two years. By then Myra had weaned the first three and was wondering about old wives. She was nineteen years old with five children. Nursing stopped nothing. She hadn't even dried up between birthings. She thought about what other women did, turning away from their husbands and all, but in the business of being married, that was the best part. Half the time she was winkin' at Everett more than he was winkin' at her. The love in The Shoe could not be denied. Now The Shoe was full.

Myra became a familiar sight at the docks. She often left her brood with Aunt Ada and carried a dinner hamper to the Mister. The excuse was food, but the reality was The Shoe was too tight. Five babies made Myra wish for no babies. That hour with the Mister somewhat restored her.

"Goodness, it's wonderful to see all of you." Myra would nod her way through the rows of accounting men. Their desks and the high backed stools were as tall as she was. Myra felt as though she was walking in a valley of flannel and suspenders. She always made sure she wore a fresh dress with bright colors and her brown, wavy hair was brushed and pulled back with a nice ribbon. She knew the smell of baby mess was not appetizing to anyone, including to her beloved Everett. He was such a good sport about all those stinks, but she wasn't about to wear them to his work.

The other accountants enjoyed her visits as much as the Mister did. She was a bright little flower that made the dinner hour quite pleasant. She started adding extra jumbles to the basket for the men. They all seemed to love that mixture of almonds, pecans, raisins and chocolate pieces all baked into one delicious desert.

"Missus Gallaway, your cookies are grand. Everett, you are one lucky husband."

Mister was proud he married such a good looking cook. Myra felt baking was a small price to pay to get away from diapers and squalling.

"Yes, sir, I am." He beamed. "My Myra is one fine wife, aren't you, honey?"

"Yes, sweetheart. Now eat your dinner. The young'uns will be fussin' soon."

Mister came in from work early one Tuesday afternoon, looking pale.

"Darling, why are you home?" Myra had just started the boil for the supper beans and rice. He ran past her, through the back door, toward the outhouse. "North, South," was all he said. She stirred the water, adding a big pinch of salt and a plop of bacon grease, glad her stomach felt settled. The North South disease was no fun.

Many minutes later, Myra realized he hadn't returned. Wiping her hands on her apron, she stepped out on the stoop. There was something in the air, an odd chill. She hugged herself as she called out. "Everett, are you still in the necessary?" Myra heard the strangest sound, a banging like a far off shutter caught in the wind. She felt her chest tighten. "Everett, do you need help?"

Silence filled the backyard, thicker than fog. Myra walked to the privy and pulled open the door. Her dear, dear husband was on the seat with his pants down, slumped sideways, covered with vomit. Stain was on the walls where he had tried to pound out a distress with his fist. His eyes were closed.

Her screams roused him enough to focus. "I don't think I can get to the house. My bowels won't stop." Those words took all his energy and he convulsed, retching again. This time the vomit was tinged with blood. The diarrhea continued.

Myra ran to the shed, scrabbled through the garden tools, and brought back the wheel barrow. She propped open the door with its front axle and entered the privy. The smell was overwhelming. Holding her breath, she pulled Everett to her, forcing him to rise. With his pants down and his shirt front foul, Myra locked her arms around his waist and waltzed him to the barrow. Holding him with her body, she hiked up his drawers and britches to preserve his dignity. Releasing him, he fell into the bed of the barrow, long legs over the sides. Everett appeared unconscious. Using all of her strength, she dragged him toward the back door. Halfway there, he messed his trousers. There was blood in that, too.

Grabbing a clean tablecloth from the clothes line, she covered him, hoping to hide his horror. Leaving him in the yard, she ran out front where she waved down the first man she saw. Myra's appearance shocked him. The dance with her husband had stained her dress and apron with his illness. Myra's gasping words confirmed her need and he readily agreed to help get Everett into the house. The stranger stayed with her until her husband was clean and put to bed wearing a fresh night shirt. The man insisted on washing his hands at the pump. Only then did he introduce himself.

"My name is Joseph Cohen. Rabbi Joe, they call me. I know your uncle Harry. Do you want me to get him for you?"

"Please. I'm too scared to leave Everett and the babies. Could you ask for my aunt Ada, too?"

"Of course, my dear." The kind man looked hard at her. "Keep your children away from their daddy. You need to wash yourself and change clothes while you can." He was very serious as he spoke. "I have seen this before. You must burn his clothes, your clothes, and that tablecloth. Don't let your children use the outhouse, just the privy closet inside."

Myra stared at him. "Cholera?"

"Probably."

By the time Uncle Harry and Aunt Ada arrived, Myra had scrubbed herself and put all soiled garments and the table cloth to flame in the fire pit. Ada took the children to her house where she kept them. Harry burned the wood of the outhouse, filled the hole, and dug a new pit. Several of Uncle Harry's Masonic Brothers wagoned over a newly built latrine. Thanks to continuous hand washing, no one else got sick, praise God. Harry and Myra tended Everett until he died, three days later. After the undertaker came, they burned everything he had soiled, including the bed ticking. Only then did the children come home.

Myra became the Widow Gallaway on Friday, her twentieth birthday. Everett left her five hungry mouths to feed and that was about all. With the help of Aunt Ada's recipes and the resilience of every woman in her bloodline, Myra went into the baking business. It was the one thing she knew how to do that could make some money. She kept Junior around for company and fetching. He had his mama's coloring, but his hair was straight like his daddy's. All the children needed barbering, but she made sure Junior was especially raggedy when she sent him to the corner store. That seemed to bring a cheaper bag of flour or a larger tin of lard. The boy had a tired, old man's look about him since his papa died, and that his face broke the shop man's heart. It worked every time, or so Myra thought, having no notion Uncle Harry made a gentlemen's arrangement for a family discount.

Myra started her selling with Mister's co-workers. Those treats she'd shared so generously from her husband's dinner basket were pleasantly remembered. Mrs. Myra Gallaway reached almost four foot nine inches in her stocking feet and she wore very high-heeled buttoned shoes so she could trick people into believing she had stature. She thought she fooled them, but she fooled no one. Everybody knew this tiny bit of a woman needed taking care of, and so they bought.

"Jumbles, plunkets, crybabies," she'd call as she walked the boardwalk to the office. At the office entrance the counting men would gather around Myra. Once inside, she'd sell her homemade cookies.

"Mrs. Gallaway, how are you? We sure are glad to see you." The men tried to remember Mister but eventually gave up. Mister was well known for his sudden death and that was about it, and his tiny woman who needed taking care of. The men loved buying cakes to support Mrs. Gallaway's dear children. Thinking about the tiny woman didn't hurt, either. It seemed the whole town knew about all those crying babies and Myra's struggles. How she did it, nobody knew.

"Your sweets look mighty fine. Y'all got any with plum jam in the middle?"

"My wife asked me to bring home the ones with raisins. Do you have any of those today?"

The room was a'buzz with chatter. No work was getting done. The office supervisor, Ike Jameson, sent Myra out to the docks with her basket after two days. She could sell to his men if there was anything left. He allowed the Widow Gallaway full access to the loading areas, requesting two cookies as passage. Myra was grateful and always gave him three, one for his Missus. Mr. Jameson ate them all as he smiled at the thought of his good deed. His wife, Julia, got his wages and, surely that was enough.

The women who walked the wharves were usually not selling baked goods. Their sassy sway described their livelihood, 'though sometimes colored girls from the fancy restaurants and fine hotels would come in with the cooks to carry out the best fish from the mongers.

The Widow Gallaway wore respectability like an apron. In fact, her ankle-length apron was her advertisement. Aunt Ada had sewn several for her with deep pockets on the front. There she put the coins from her sales. She was a picture of propriety with her black bonnet, her basket of wares, and her starched white apron covering her widow's weeds. As time passed, Myra learned to walk in such a way so the discrete jingle of coins could be heard as she stepped. This just might remind the sailors of her five poor, hungry babies.

Only whores were allowed on the ships, so Myra had to call out her presence on the docks louder than the noise of the working men.

"Jumbles. Plunkets. Crybabies." She turned her call into a plea at the end by saying 'cry' just a bit more pathetic and a whine added to 'babieeees'. The wharf men and sailors would gather with their money and she would sell her sweets in nothing flat. How those men loved to look at a respectable widow. Myra would smile, lower her lashes and talk about her children. Sometimes she would speak all their names, listing out Junior, the twins Benjy and Franky, Theo, and Nora Lee. For most of the time, though, she just called them 'Babies'. The stories really helped with the sales.

For a while Aunt Ada watched the children, but when that stopped, the children were put out daily to anyone who felt charitable. That didn't last long. Charity comes with a price.

Myra became the talk of the neighborhood. Bless her heart for her situation, but enough was getting to be enough. What did she do out there on those wharves? Was she selling more than sweets? The tongues had begun and no respectable housewife was going to keep Myra's children so she could walk the wharves, selling who-knows-what.

Chapter 2

THE FLOCK

Aunt Ada

Uncle Harry and Aunt Ada Dickenson leased and ran the local mercantile building since 'God grew hair', as Aunt Ada would say. The sign out front read 'Dickenson's Grocery, Dry Goods, and Masonic Temple'. The part of the sign that had been next to the Masonic Temple used to say 'Upstairs', but it had long ago rotted and broke off. Uncle Harry never fixed it because the Masons knew where to go anyway.

Aunt Ada had the biggest heart, and Uncle Harry realized her kindly handouts were seriously hurting the till.

"Now, woman," he began. Ada knew when he said *now woman* something serious was fixin' to happen. She smoothed back her curly white hair, reset her comb, and looked at him straight on, arms folded in front of her ample bosom. He looked straight back.

"Now, woman, you know we are not running accounts longer than six months. Why is it that every time I settle the weeklies, I see so many over-dues? I think you write 'on account' more than you write the word 'paid'. You are giving away the store."

"Darlin'," she drawled. "You know some people require more. Some families are in need."

"Then some families can go find work and cover their bills." He harrumphed, stomping out to light a cigar. After a hot cup from the ever-present coffee pot slow-boiling on the backroom stove, he returned with a plan. Running his fingers through his thick silver hair, he put his arms around his wife.

"I want you to take a break from the store. I know

you have a kind soul, but we are in the business of sellin', not givin'. Would you like to spend more time at the church? I could talk to Brother O'Bryan about his daughter, Sulee. She might could use the work helping out here."

"Darlin', you know best." She relaxed in his arms. Ada didn't let on, but she knew she would be really happy with this arrangement. She realized a long time ago that working with and being a wife to your husband could lead to double-duty troubles. Now she'd have more time to help with The Shoe, and, unlike him, the Church Guild would not fuss at her for being too kind hearted.

The Guild

In town it was another story. The Methodist women of South Lowman Street were damn tired of keeping Myra Gallaway's snot-nosed brats. When Mr. Gallaway died, there was sympathy all around, however when her Aunt Ada felt obliged to spend more time at the church doing the Lord's work and Myra ended up farming out those children, the gossip was runnin' full force.

Julia Jameson carried home to her husband what he already knew about Myra's situation. The thought of having to work to feed a family appalled her. Shaking her finger at her husband, that evening she laid down the law.

"You are never to impede that poor woman's honest support of her children, but if you notice the clerks are spending clocked time visiting with her as they buy their sweets, you better just watch out for the dock master. Shirked work could cost you your job. Then there'll be hell to pay."

Mr. Jameson thought he was paying it anyway, being married to Julia. He didn't want to owe a debt to hell, to Julia, or to the dock master, so he just smiled and ate all three cookies.

"Yes, dear," he said.

"That baby girl of hers is a terror. Just the other day I saw her lift her dress above her knees and run with those boys. Then, right there in the yard, she did her wee-wee." Mrs. Gaithers sipped her coffee and continued. "I have no idea if she even had on drawers. It's no wonder she doesn't know how to behave."

"I think that boy Junior is more of a mother than Myra is," tisked Mrs. Wallace.

The ladies of South Lowman were gathered for coffee and cake, a daily ritual. Today was not Guild, so they were at the home of Mrs. Christopoulis, the only Greek in the neighborhood. The house was full of those funny statues and pictures, but the women forgave her heritage and her religion once they tasted her honey cakes. Besides, they all felt so sophisticated to claim a foreigner as a neighbor.

"All five of them could use a good face washing. You'd think she'd see how dirty they are."

"At least they're clean for Sunday School. I'll bet Ada has a hand in that." The women spoke over each other as they gossiped.

"All those children...thank heavens we are not animals," said Julia, taking a bite of, what did they call it? black lava? "We do not rut, do we, dears? Civilized women do not have five children." The ladies all agreed. Civilized women controlled their men 'that way'. Civilized women allowed men to take care of their needs elsewhere. At least some of them did. Others used the vinegar sponge and prayer. Often those women became too busy with family for coffee and cake and dropped out of the group.

Miss Annie and her sisters

Miss Annie Hoffen would sometimes join them, accompanied by her sisters Mrs. Wallace and Mrs. Gaithers. Annie was the only unmarried woman in the

15

group. She wasn't just an unmarried woman, she was an old maid living with the burden of caring for her very cantankerous mother.

Mother couldn't get over the anger at her husband for being such a fool to answer the call of the militia. Others often wondered if Otto left in self-defense, figurin' fighting the wildest native was a preference to his house full of hard-willed women. The romance of Indian chasing was cut short when the cavalry, led by Captain Dawson, met up with the likes of Chief Victorio at Las Animas Creek. There Otto was buried along with the others. Mother never forgave him and took to her bed, where she died twenty-some years later. The two younger girls eventually found husbands and the house-care was left to Annie. Mother was moved into the parlor where she spent most of her time sleeping and complaining.

Annie realized her mother had long been taking Lydia Pinkham's Compound. By adding a bit of Mrs. Winslow's Soothing Syrup to the tonic, her mother found sleep quickly. The doctor approved and directed her to administer the potion several times a day as needed. Peace reigned.

Miss Annie was forever grateful for Mother's medicine. Her sisters agreed, along with their husbands, that Mother and Annie could best be supported with pooled finances. Having seen what some widows had to do, the family offered monthly help. While Mother slept, Annie was able to represent herself socially with some comfort. Mother's daily nap came at high heat after dinner and she would sleep until four-thirty, give or take some minutes. High heat meant no one came calling and that is when Mr. Wilson could.

Mr. Carlton Wilson had been an early business associate of her father. The two men owned a grist mill at one time and their wives became friends. When Mrs. Wilson died in the stillbirth of her first child, Mr. Carl turned to Otto for solace. Mr. Carl became the brother Otto wished he had. Mother started setting a nightly place at the dinner table for him because she knew Carl would show up anyway. His sadness was lifted as he looked on the sweet, plain faces of his ready-made family. He was welcomed and appreciated until Father decided to go off and get himself killed. Mr. Carl knew it would be wrong to sit at a husbandless table, and he quietly slipped out of the lives of the Hoffen women. Time passed and Mother took to her bed. The young ones grew up and married while Annie managed.

Then one day there was a knock on the back door. Annie answered.

"Miss Annie, do you remember me?"

Annie stared hard, the afternoon sun glaring her eyes. "Is it Mr. Wilson?"

"Yes ma'am, it is."

She recognized the voice, but not the face. He was so different. He was a gentleman.

"Oh, my goodness, please come in," and that is how it started. While Mother napped Mr. Wilson told Annie about his life these many years. After Father left, Mr. Wilson struggled to find his aim. He sold the mill, traveled north to Houston and went to work in the supply business. Houston was becoming the railroad center of Texas, moving the cotton north. Carl watched and learned. Little by little he got his hands into the works of providing food for all of those railroad men. He took what remained of the mill money and invested in a small commissary that sold the flour for the bread the men needed. He blushed as he spoke of his success.

"Miss Annie, I have a bank draft for your mother. I took your father's half of the grist money and put it in my new business. It has more than tripled and I want to get right with this."

"Oh Mr. Carl, may I call you that? Mother's an

invalid and is a' bed in the parlor. She will be so thrilled when she wakes from her nap. We had no idea there was anything left from the mill."

"Please call me Carl. Yes, the money has done quite well. Please look."

When Annie opened the folded draft, she couldn't breathe. The cheque was made out to her mother for the unbelievable sum of five thousand dollars. That was seven years' wages for a skilled craftsman. She caught her breath, folded the paper and handed it back to Mr. Wilson. He stared at her.

"Sir, do not toy with us." She turned and walked past him out the back door, leaving him standing there, dumbfounded. Once on the stoop, she began to cry.

"Miss Annie, wait. Please stop." Mr. Wilson was standing beside her, his hand patting her arm. "This draft is true. Your father invested in the mill fair and square. Consider this his legacy." He took Annie by the shoulders and turned her to face him. "Your father was my best friend. I minded his money and now I honor him. Please take your inheritance." He took out his handkerchief and wiped her cheeks. She let him.

Mother felt it was best to have the money deposited in Mr. Wilson's bank in upstate La Porte with Carl as trustee and they never spoke of it again. They both knew once Mother was gone, the brothers-in-law may not be so generous in their support of Annie. The women agreed this windfall would be Annie's keep later on.

Mr. Wilson started calling on the Hoffen household whenever he was in town with the pretense of checking on the family of his old friend. He quickly realized the scheduling of Mother's doses and used that time to court Annie. It took a while for the daughter to realize what was going on. Annie always knew she was plain and had never liked the way her nose beaked. She thought she was the least attractive of the sisters, even though general consensus in the Guild room differed. Now she was relaxing into the happiness of having a beau for the first time in her life, even if no one knew. She and Carl would sit at the kitchen table over tea and lemon water and he would talk his business. He so appreciated how she listened and seemed to have the right advice. Even though he was many years her senior, he was a man of vigor and spirit and she loved their tabletop conversations. He admired her strength. Eventually that tabletop became a place to hold hands and make secret plans.

Sitting at the table, he proposed late that summer. The ring was an emerald surrounded with small diamonds.

"Yes, my dear, yes, but we must wait until Mother joins Daddy."

"Would you consider allowing us all to live together? We would wed and then I would move the both of you upstate into my house. I have plenty of room."

"Oh Carlton, you have no idea what it is like when Mother is awake. She can be so horrid." Annie held his hands tightly. "My mother refuses to do anything for herself. Even though she is quite strong, she won't walk to the necessary. Excuse me for saying this, but I don't think you should be expected to be involved with emptying the bedside privy chair. Please don't get me started about bathing her. Sometimes she tries to smack me when I bring the basin and cloth. When she doesn't like her food, she spits or screams and then throws it at me. Oh, my dear, let us wait until I am free to give you all my attention."

Mr. Wilson agreed and slipped the ring on her left hand. Leaning across, he gave her their very first kiss. Annie got up and walked to his side of table.

"Please stand. We are engaged and I need a proper kiss." He did just that. Twice.

Once Carl left, Annie took the ring and threaded it on the gold chain that held her cross. She would not wear it on her finger until a proper announcement could be made.

She had no idea when that would be. "Oh my stars and buttons, what have I done now?" She began to cry tears of hope for the first time in her life. She was going to become a Missus. She wore that chain for several years, waiting on Mother.

Chapter 3

THE SHOE

Almost seven-year-old Junior Gallaway had the continuous task of young'un watching since his mama had to go to work selling sweets. This was very hard on the boy. Franky was toilet trained but slow at growing and needed extra watching. The youngest ones were just learning how to use the necessary. Junior knew his duty, but, dag-nab-it, changin' those diapers was tiresome. Without telling his mother, he started sitting Theo and Nora Lee on the pot at the same time.

Nora was easy 'cause she peed straight down. He'd hold them both so they didn't fall, poke Theo's wing-ding down between his legs and wait. The sound of the first dribble got the other one going. Junior would sing, "Tinkle, tinkle, little one, poop some more and then you're done." It became the first tune those two ever sang. Junior was just glad to be getting them in drawers.

The standin' up part became interesting. Junior took Theo and the potty out back. He set it by the bushes 'cause he wasn't up to cleaning the floor from the bad aimin'. Naturally Nora Lee came along.

"Watch. You're gonna learn howta' put out a fire." He lit a kitchen match and dropped it into the pot. Then Junior undid his fly, pulled out his hose and pointed it at the pot. PSSSS. The fire was out. "Now you do it." Junior buttoned up, and put Theo in place.

"He ain't gonna do it. You didn't make a fire." Nora stood there, shaking her head, all sassy-fied.

"You hush up, girly, I'm doing the best I can. I was just showin' him how to drain his tube. Bet you can't do any better." Junior did not have the patience or the time for her buttin' into boy stuff.

"Light a match. It's only fair he puts out a fire, too."

"I want fire. I want fire." Theo seemed to realize that pee-potting might be fun, after all.

"All right already. Just get out your dingle and be ready." Junior dumped the pot in the bushes and set it back in place. However it was still wet, and after four matches the fire brigade gave up. Theo ended up hitting the target anyway and the match sticks started to float.

"Watch me, watch me." The boys turned around to see Nora Lee. She had opened her drawers and was standing there with her skirt hiked. "Them matches are gonna float like the big boats Mama sees." With the boys watching, she squatted over the pot. By the time she was done, the children agreed she was the winner of the pee-pee contest. Junior was just glad Mama didn't see them. She'd have been mad at him for wasting matches.

One Saturday afternoon mid-December, Myra was spending rare time mopping her kitchen floor. She already hung the wash. Good God, how she hated wash-day. Everybody knew Monday was wash-day, but Mondays were her best sellin' days, so, just like everything else that happened at her house, she continued to fuel the gossips. The children were who-knows-where and that was all right with her. *Here's hoping they stay gone 'til those boards dry.* She was sitting on the front stoop steps with her morning coffee, hard-boiled, when she heard Nora Lee hollering. It wasn't the 'I'm hurt' holler, it was the tattle-tale holler. Being the baby and the only girl, Nora Lee learned long ago how to get the others riled. Myra was wise to her but the boys weren't. She sat waiting, elbows on her knees with a white china mug in hand, to see what was next.

"Maamaa," Nora Lee whined. The back screen slammed.

Damn that child, she's running through the kitchen.

"Maamaa, Franky's been playing at the pump." The child crashed out the front screen and plopped down by her mother.

"And…" Myra smoothed the child's ringlets out of her eyes. *Where was her ribbon?*

"Now he's covered."

"With what?"

"With ashes." Nora Lee looked far too satisfied.

"Ashes? How?" Things were beginning to dawn on Myra. She set down her coffee and stood up. "Is he in the ash pit?" Her wet wash was hanging close proximity.

"Yes, Mama. You gonna get him?"

"Missy that is not your concern." Myra was already heading around the side of the house. "You stay put. I don't need you pokin' into this."

Nora Lee skittered around the other side of the house. There Franky sat, right in the middle of the fenced fire ring. He was making mountains, as happy as any four year old had a right to be.

"Frank Elwin Gallaway, what do you think you are doing?" Myra stood outside the cold fire cage with her hands on her hips.

"Makin' hills." Her least'n smiled up at her, all ashes and love.

"Look at yourself, boy." Myra had lost her patience when Nora Lee smeared the kitchen floor. This was just too much. "You are filthy, child. It's stuck to you from one end to the other. Your face is covered. Were you in the water?"

"Uh huh." Franky stood up and noticed himself for the first time. He started to sniffle.

"I sorry. I sorry. Don't 'pank me Mama. Don't 'pank me."

"I am not going to spank you, young man. I am going to bathe you."

"Oh, Mama, don't bathe me, 'pank me." He sneezed, sending ashes and snot everywhere, including on the wet whites. With more energy than was needed, Myra reached into to wire cage and jerked her son up and out.

Right there, for all the world to see, she stripped the boy to jaybird status. Leaving soaked, nasty clothes behind, she hauled sobbing Franky straight to the pump. Down went the boy, whoosh went the water, and Myra kept the handle going long after the ashes were rinsed.

"Maamaa, he's turnin' blue." The ever observant Nora Lee brought her mother back from the rage that kept the handle in motion. "Maamaa, his teeth are chatterin'."

"Miss Nosey Rosey, I told you to stay on the porch, but since you're here, go get me a rag, soap, and a towel." Myra picked up her shivering, snot dripping boy and carried him to the back stoop. Nora Lee reappeared with the supplies. "Go find the rest and I'll do everybody now, since it is Saturday." After cold backyard baths for all, she let Franky's clothes dry ashy. All she could hope was to shake 'em after they came off the line. Myra was too tired and frustrated to do anything else.

That night Franky started to cough. All five children slept in the same room. As the only girl, Nora Lee was given the trundle. However most nights she would snuggle in with Junior and Theo. The twins shared the other bed and they would talk themselves to sleep. Myra figured those two started this in the womb and it wasn't going to stop now.

"Mama, Franky won't be quiet." Benjy was standing by his mama's bed in his nightshirt. It was really dark outside and it took a bit for Myra to swim to the surface.

"Just don't talk to him." She hadn't wanted to open her eyes. Sleep was so precious.

"Mama, you should hear him. He's coughin', not talkin'." Benjy was shaking her shoulder. "Mama, he's sick."

Myra sat up and listened. Benjy was right. His twin was not only coughing, he sounded like he was choking. Nightgown flying, Myra was to the bedside of her child before you could say 'boo'. The choking stopped and he was gasping. His little chest was pullin' in and out, trying to catch a breath. Myra snatched him into a bear hug and started rocking him. After what seemed like forever, he finally calmed into a proper rhythm of air in, air out.

"Baby, baby, what happened?" His color was gray, scary gray, like when he was born. "Oh darling baby, Mama's here." He had silently cuddled against her, his head on her breast. The heavy coughing started again. Pulling the top quilt up over them, she sat there on the edge of the bed, rocking him until daybreak, remembering...everything. Benjy fell asleep, curled around her back under the covers. His arm was around her waist, touching his brother.

At first light she disentangled Benjy, stood with her beloved in her arms, and walked into her own room. Carefully balancing the gasping child on her bed, she got herself dressed. Using one hand to steady Franky, she put her housedress over her nightgown, not bothering with her corset. Slipping into her shoes, she wrapped the child in her day shawl, gathered him up and walked out of the house. Junior met her on the porch.

"Oh, my big boy, why are you up?"

"I could hear him. Is he breathing?"

"Not much. I'm going to Aunt Ada. She'll know what to do."

Junior stood there, staring. "You won't let him die, will you, Mama? Auntie and Uncle live awful far away."

"Oh darling child, I won't let him die. You tell the others when they wake up. I don't guess we will make it to Sunday School today. I love you."

"Hurry Mama. I love you, too."

She knew she couldn't run with him. That would wear her out quicker than anything. Myra took a deep breath. There it was again, that odd chill. Holding her bundle close, she headed out with long strides. The rhythm of Myra's walk seemed to calm Franky. He was breathing without the cough, soft in, soft out. Turning the corner by the Dickenson's house, Myra was beginning to feel safe. Franky stirred in her arms. Suddenly he went still, arched his back, and opened his mouth wide. No sound. No air. Myra ran.

"No. No. No. Breathe, baby breathe." She raced up the walk and crashed into the front screen. Myra put her mouth on Franky's and blew, all the while kicking the front screen. Kick, kick, kick, blow. *Oh God, no.* Kick, kick, blow. The child was limp in her arms.

The front door opened and there stood Uncle Harry in his long johns. His hair was all a'tossle and he was not looking his usual happy self.

"Who's out there wakin' the dead? Sunday is a day of rest, dammit." Then he focused through the screen.

"Jesus, child, what happened?" Over his shoulder he shouted. "Ada, get down here. Don't dress, just get here now!" He pushed open the screen and took Franky in his arms.

"Blow in him. He's quit breathing." Myra gasped the words. In two steps, he had the child laid out on the dining room table. "Coughing, choking all night. Stopped breathing at the corner." Was she making any sense? *Oh dear God, save my baby.*

Harry put his mouth over his great nephew's and softly blew. Nothing. He blew a little harder. Franky's chest rose. Ada was beside her niece, holding her as they watched their precious darlin' on that table. Harry blew again. Chest up and then down. One more blow. Chest up, down, up, down. The child began to cough. *Yes, baby, yes.*

Ada elbowed herself in front of Harry and sat Franky straight up on the table. He was wide-eyed, staring. Ada pounded his back, hard. Franky blinked and started to cry a sound that reminded his mama of the birthing, his weak baby squawks. Myra started crying, sobbing, gasping, trying to suck in the air her beloved needed. She pulled her dress over her head, exposing herself through the thin fabric of her nightgown. Reaching down, she slid the boy off of the table, turned him around, and put his quivering chest tightly against hers.

"Mama's got you," she whispered to him. "Mama's breathing for you. Feel Mama? You can do it too." Myra took in giant gulps, expanding her chest so that Franky could feel her.

"Feel Mama breathe, my darling. Feel Mama breathe." With one arm around his bottom and the other across his back, she held him against her, continuously whispering. His chest started to take the rhythm of her movements and soon Franky was no longer gray. Uncle Harry lifted the boy out of Myra's arms, and gave him the biggest smooch on the cheek.

"Come on son, let's find me some britches and you something cool to drink. You like lemonade?" He looked at Myra. "Better put your dress on. Doc's on his way."

***

Ada grabbed her housecoat and headed out for Dr. McKnight as soon as Myra pulled the baby to her chest. It wasn't until Hazel McKnight let her in did Ada realize she'd been rushing with bare feet. Doc had his old mare harnessed almost as fast as Hazel found a pair of shoes and shawl for Ada.

Hazel handed the doctor his kit, gave both of them a quick kiss, and away they went. Ada filled him in on what she knew, which wasn't much. The child stopped breathing after coughing and choking through the night. Dr. McKnight listened, his mind working on a cause. *It damn well better not be whooping cough. That could wipe out all of them.* He snapped his whip above the horse's head and spoke.

"Did Myra say if any of the others were coughing? What about the twin? Is he well?" The carriage was pulling to a stop at the front of the house.

"Myra didn't say a thing about any of the others. I think she would have if they were sick. Here, give me the reins. I'll do the hitch."

Doc ran up the porch steps, two at a time, and didn't even stop to knock. What he saw was not what he expected. Franky was sitting on the settee with a glass of lemonade in his hand. There was a plate of cookies by his side with one tightly held, half-eaten treat in his hand. Then he saw Harry and Myra. Their appearances were all Doc needed. He set down his kit and gestured for Myra to step into the kitchen.

"Tell me, Mother, why I am here?" Dr. McKnight called all of his mother's 'Mother'. "Which one is this one, the first or second?"

"Second. Franky."

"I remember that one. Sure surprised me. I recall that he was a bit frail. So, what happened?"

Myra told him about how Benjy woke her, how she sat with Franky until daybreak, and the trek to her aunt and uncle's house for help. She told about the child stopping breathing and how they blew the breath back into him. She even told him about how she held him to her chest, willing him the rhythm of life. Then Myra started to cry again. He handed her his handkerchief. He found his Mothers often needed one when their children were ailing, so he carried several.

"Are any others sick? How were they yesterday?"

"No." She wiped her eyes and sniffed. "They all seemed fine. After Franky got out of the ash pit, they had baths and played in the house. It was a good evening."

Doc was checking to see if Ada had her morning coffee going yet. She hadn't. He stopped and turned.

"Say that again."

"Which part?" Myra was staring at him.

"Did you say Franky was in the ash pit? How long? Was he covered? What about his face?" Doc was already heading back to the parlor. Myra scrambled to follow.

"Yes. Don't know. Yes. Yes."

Doc opened his case, took out his stethoscope and put in the ear pieces. He sat down beside Franky. "Is the lemonade good? May I taste?" He took the glass from the boy and nodded for Harry to take it to the other room.

Harry picked up the plate of cookies and handed them both to Myra with a wink. "Your Auntie's done with the horse. I don't think she'd appreciate knowin' we were eating in the parlor." Myra carried them to the kitchen sideboard.

"Remember when I listened to you with this when all of you came in my office?" Franky smiled at Dr. McKnight. "We're going to do it again. Is that all right with you?" The child nodded.

"Take a big boy breath. That's good. Do it again. Aha, I thought so." He opened his case to put away the instrument and to get his sack of cough candy. Suddenly Franky started up again. Ada rushed into the room from the porch. Doc turned to the adults and motioned to them to stay still. Then he pulled up the boy's night shirt and watched his bird-like chest, heaving and quivering. He put the stethoscope against his back, listening as the spasms subsided. He took a bottle of Dr. Seth Arnold's Cough Cure from his kit.

"Missus Ada, please bring me a small glass of water and a spoon. Then I need you to set your kettle to boil. While you're at it, make some coffee. We're going to be here a while. Brother Harry, I need an oilcloth. Missus Myra, I am going to try to save this child. Do you know if he inhaled any ash?" Dr. McKnight looked intently at the child's chest movements while he gave orders and asked questions.

"I recollect so, come to think about it. When I caught him in the pit, he started to cry. The snot runnin' down his chin was full of ashes. I just thought the mess was from his face, he was so dirty."

"I think Franky has ash in his lungs. If we don't get him cleaned out, he could get pneumonia. That would be very bad. As it is, y'all better pray that we're not too late." Dr. McKnight looked grave. "This here boy started out peaked. We have to keep an extra close eye on him." He looked around for Ada. "Mother, go check on that hot water and send in your Auntie."

Ada walked out of the kitchen with the glass and spoon. "What do you need, Doctor?"

"First of all, I need for you to get some clothes on."

Ada looked at herself and blushed. She was still in her housecoat, Hazel's shoes and shawl. "Yes sir. Good idea."

"Then you are to take the rig. You can drive a carriage, can't you?" Ada nodded. "Go to my house. Get my wife and take her to the Gallaway's to check on the rest of the children. Tell her to use my other stethoscope and listen to their chests. If there are any sick ones, tell her to bring them all here. Get Myra some proper clothes. I noticed that she seemed to be missing some things." The doctor measured out a spoon of syrup and stirred it into the water.

"Here, son, drink this. It will help you." Franky dutifully swallowed the medicine, making a face at its bitterness.

Ada dressed quicker 'n a lick, kissed Franky on the forehead and was gone with the carriage before the coffee was done. Uncle Harry came in carrying the oilcloth from the kitchen table.

"Water's starting to boil. Here's the kitchen table cover. Is it big enough? Tell me Brother, what do you have in mind?"

"I'll tell you both over coffee. Missus Myra, is the jamoke ready? Does your auntie have any more of those cookies?" Doc McKnight turned back to his patient. He was now lying down on the settee, head propped up on his auntie's favorite satin pillow, the rose colored one with the embroidered angels. Franky looked hopefully at the doctor when he heard the word 'cookies'. "Yes, son, you may have one." Franky smiled, eyelids drooping. The medicine was working. Soon the child was snoring, that wonderful sound of life.

"Brother Harry," Doc said after his first cookie and the top half cup of coffee. "I need for you to build a small tent with the oilcloth. You are going to save that baby with a cigar." Everyone stared at him. He took another sweet and washed it down with the rest of his brew. Myra filled his cup back up and waited.

The plan was to put Franky in the tent with his Uncle Harry puffing a big stogie, making the child breath the smoke. Hopefully the boy would start to cough and choke, bringing up the ashes in his lungs. As soon as the fit was slowing down, Ada would sit him at the table, still coughing. She was to put a bowl of steaming salt water in front of him and a tea towel over his head. Breathing the steam should, hopefully, wash the ash out. This treatment, along with syrup doses, needed to be done every few hours for two days.

"Brother, can this young'un stay with you and Ada until Wednesday? I have a feeling Missus Myra doesn't smoke cigars." The doctor turned to Myra. "Your baby will be safe here, you know that. If it isn't the ashes and something else, your others don't need to get sick, if they aren't already. All we can do is wait and see."

Ada returned several hours later, bearing corset and fresh clothes for Myra and a clean night shirt and drawers for Franky.

"Doctor, your Hazel checked the others and heard nothing but healthy chests. She has them all with her now."

Ada poured herself a hot cup and told the story. The children were so frantic. While she was answering their questions and fixing breakfast for the brood, Mrs. McKnight supervised young'un dressing.

"I know your mama said no Sunday School. I'm taking you anyway." As she spoke, Hazel was checking shirt tails while Ada was lick-slicking the boys' hair. Nora Lee was starting to rumble into one of her fits. "We," continued the good doctor's wife, "will be riding in my carriage."

Nora Lee was first dressed, brushed, and standing by the horse. "You boys better get your hats on, isn't that right, Mrs. McKnight? I got mine on."

"Yes, dear, the boys are dressed, but first we have to take your Aunt Ada back home."

"Girls in front, boys in back. Who has their Bible?" called Ada as she shut the front door. With Nora Lee wedged between the women and the three others squeezed in the back, they made a fine, but noisy parade to the Dickenson's house. Myra heard them before they came to a full stop.

"Dear God, she's bringing them here. Oh, Doctor, that means they're all sick."

"Not with that noise. You go and see."

Myra ran out to the carriage and offered a hand to her aunt. Ada stepped down and nodded, giving quick assurance that everything was fine. Myra turned to the children. "You all be good for Mrs. McKnight, you hear me? You gotta pray for your brother, that's most important. Missus Hazel, Are they well?"

"Very."

"Please take them home after services. They are not allowed to be here."

"Don't you worry. I'll keep them with me. Tell my husband they have clear chests."

"I will. Thank you."

Hazel shushed the boys, clicked her tongue at the horse, and was gone. Myra waved until she couldn't see them anymore. *God bless that woman.* She felt calm as she walked back into the house. Harry was telling his wife all about the treatment plan and the doctor was packing up his kit.

"I'm leaving you the syrup," said Dr. McKnight. "After today, only use a half spoon full. Missus Ada, don't you go fussin' at my Brother here about cigar smoke in the house. It's for the good of the child. Missus Myra, you keep the others at home, you hear? This is going to be a very busy house for a few days and your aunt and uncle do not need any more children around."

"Yes, sir." Myra tiptoed tall and gave the doctor a hug. "Thank you, thank you, thank you."

"We're not there yet." Dr. McKnight turned to Ada. "The boy is only to have warm tea and bread sop for the next day. If the coughing gets worse, stop the bread. Then if you feel it's safe, start the sop again. If all goes well, he'll be hungry for food on Wednesday. I'll be by on Thursday morning, if not before."

The family waved good-bye as the doctor headed toward home, swinging his bag. "Well," said Ada. "I've got a dinner to make. Who would like some cold roast?"

The tent treatment worked. Franky snotted his lungs clean thanks to Uncle Harry's cigars and Aunt Ada's steam and lovin'. Myra put the fear of God in the rest of them, threatening their very lives if they snuck off to see their brother. By Thursday afternoon, Dr. McKnight declared Franky well enough to go home and The Shoe was full again.

That horrible ash pit held the memories of cholera and the attack on her baby's lungs. Myra solemnly promised her brood that she would beat from here to kingdom come any child that got near those ashes again. They wisely took her advice. That willow switch was something to reckon with.

Chapter 4

JULIA

Julia Jameson fancied herself the most proper Christian woman of all the wives in the congregation. Her husband, Ike, was the boss of the counting office and she was the boss of him. Her work with the Methodist Women's Benevolence Guild was well known, considered the best next to Ada Dickenson. It was also known that Ada was doing the Good Lord's work to get away from raisin' what she had not birthed. Everyone realized that, and felt Jesus would understand, too.

What no one knew was the fact that Julia could not forgive Ike for being a deceiving Jewish bastard. She hated him to the depth of her Christian soul. Isaac Jacoby arrived in Galveston by way of Brooklyn, New York. Somewhere along the trail he got the mixin' religion and renamed himself Ike Jameson. By the time he hit Texas he was from the Dutch country of Pennsylvania.

"My foster parents were such good folk," he explained. "My guardian, I called her Mother Amelia, was a kind, simple woman, God rest her soul. I just loved her home cooked noodles." Ike's story was that he was an orphan raised by honest folks, taught to farm, read, write, and to love Our Lord Jesus Christ. He set out to seek his fortune, much to the heartbreak of his Lutheran family back on the farm. He got his funny way of talking from those hardworking people. Ike called it Dutchy, but his accent was really part Yiddish, part Brooklyn, with a dollop of rail traveling thrown in. Ike only hoped no one in Galveston had ever been to Lancaster.

Truth be told, he was put out on his own from the tenements of New York when he was fourteen because he ate too much and his mother was pregnant again by another disappearing schmuck. "Write when you get work," were

34

the last words Isaac heard from her as he walked down the street. He never did.

His Bubbe made sure he went to school, but she died when he was twelve. Isaac got his book learning at P.S. 34, where he found a love of numbers and kisses from Esther, the fast girl across the hall from Bubbe's flat. He jumped a train and got a world of livin' learnin' from the hoboes. Those two educations did Ike just fine as he talked his way into and eventually running the accounting office.

He courted Miss Julia Marie Smythe, late of Galveston, and the ceremony was fine. It was in their wedding bed that his origins were revealed in their most Biblical manner. By then it was too late.

Julia Marie Smythe Jameson had her own secrets, too. Julia was born Flossie Mae Ledbetter deep in the heart of the Texas panhandle. She was oldest of the two surviving children born to Johnnie Mae and Cletus B. Ledbetter.

"That B stands for Big Man," her daddy used to say, but Flossie Mae didn't believe him. He was short, bowlegged, and meaner'n a dog with rabies. Maybe the B stood for Bullshit. He sure was full of that. Her little brother, the one that lived, was renamed CB. Daddy decided to do the changin' sometime after the others died, and his birthed name was soon forgotten. Oh, how she loved the boy. Flossie was always glad CB was too young to remember the awful day when they had beets for supper.

Three year old Flossie was spinning circles in the kitchen. She'd just recently realized her skirt would fly out around her and she was in the middle of a cloud. She could be an angel.

"Look, Mama, see my wings."

"Yes, child, you are my angel."

Johnnie Mae was busy cleaning the beets. She had baby CB strapped to her back. That wouldn't last much longer, 'cause he was one load of a toddler, and was wantin' to start his walkin'. The water was boiling on the stove. The steam told her the wood fire in the oven was almost hot enough. She would bake the beets and boil the tops. That would be the whole meal with corn bread, fresh made while the beets cooked. No meat tonight. Cletus was sitting at the table drinking the whiskey that should have been their roast beef. He had been at it all afternoon. Johnnie Mae knew there would be nothing but garden food for a while. It was times like this causin' her to wonder what in the hell she ever did see in that man.

"Watch, Daddy. Watch me fly." Flossie began to sing as she twirled arms out wide. She made up the words as she sang to the tune of 'Jesus Loves Me'.

"I'm an angel, this I know, 'cause my wings can fly me so."

"Shut up. You ain't no angel. Yer jist a stupid, noisy girl. Jist like yer ma, all stupid and noise." Cletus took another swig of the evening's supper meat. Flossie stuck out her tongue when she turned her back. Johnnie Mae gave her a look that said, 'You better watch it, Miss Cheeky'. The singing and the spinning continued. Johnnie Mae dropped the tops into the boiling pot and went out back to pour the cleaning water on the cabbages.

"You can't quit me singin' my song. I will sing it all day long."

Cletus stood. He had to steady himself. He took a step toward the child.

"You shut up yer mouth, or I'll shut it fer ya." He was fumbling for his belt.

Flossie stopped still. She knew what the belt meant. He used it on her when she wet her drawers. She started walking backwards. He pulled the belt loose. That's when it happened.

Her little self was just tall enough. The cast iron stove front said MIZE & SILLIMAN. At first she didn't feel it. Then she screamed. Her back was on fire. There was a Z burnt into her dress. Cletus grabbed her arm.

"You stupid brat. Look wha' chu done. You done ruint yer dress. Your mama's gonna whup you." Flossie was screaming even louder. "Shut up. I tol' you to shut up. You ain't ever gonna learn to shut up. I'll teach you, you baby bitch." Cletus jerked the smoldering dress up over her head. Holding tight to her tiny arm, he used the belt where it would do the most good, on her back, right by the blistering. He might never would have stopped except Johnnie Mae came runnin' in with the wash basin and clobbered him a good one. She shifted the baby, gathered up her precious girl and ran her to the stream, laying her flat on her back in the water. It was a long time before mother and child stopped crying.

The Z was branded between her shoulder blades, but not centered. The stripes were every which way down her back. It should have faded, hoping to disappear. That didn't happen. Her three year old mind kept that whole mess deep down. However, Cletus did teach his lesson. Flossie learned grown men like to hurt you and you better never love one.

Her baby brother CB was sent to the ships when he was nine and she was eleven. Oh, how she grieved his going. He was her hero. Somebody in that house had to be. CB looked like Daddy with his bow legs, but he sure enough didn't have his temperament. He worked hard to keep her away from all the stuff that was going on between the grown-ups, even though he was so small. Later Daddy told how CB was on the trade routes from Galveston to Shreveport, traveling to Panama and back again. Flossie would think of all his adventures. He was the strongest, smartest sailor on the ship, even if he was only nine years old. Her school teacher gave her an old Atlas. Flossie called it her study book. She wore out the page of the Gulf of Mexico, tracing his route and dreaming.

Johnnie Mae invested all her Mama time in Flossie.

She knew, with the right training, Flossie could pass into society and find a husband with straight legs and a kindly disposition. She bought *The Behavior Book: A Manual For Ladies* by Miss Eliza Leslie. With determination, elocution lessons from the local librarian, and the family's penchant for name changing, the new Julia Marie Smythe lost her country talk and her Ledbetter history.

Johnnie Mae took sick 'round about then. Her last words were whispered to Flossie.

"Baby Child. You are fifteen. You are ready to be a lady. I have money hidden in a coffee can inside the old dead tree by the creek. Git out of this house tonight. Run, my Baby, run. Don't let your daddy see you. Don't let your daddy stop you. Go to the main road and head south. My time is soon. I love you."

She did as she was told. She eventually landed in Galveston with thoughts of her brother and walked into the first Protestant church she saw.

"Excuse me, Reverend. My name is Julia and I need your help." She stood in the main office, trembling.

"Um, er, are you in trouble with a boy?"

"Oh, no." Julia burst into tears. "I had to run away. Please, please, can you help me?" Julia told the minister about the convent school she attended. They were insisting she become a Bride of Jesus. Could he please find shelter for her?

She was taken in by Reverend Nicholson's wife, Linda Sue, and put to board in their extra room, all paid for by the church. Her fine speech was evidence enough concerning her convent education. Besides no Protestant minister in his right mind would return this delightful young lady to the Catholics. Julia eventually evolved into the local Methodist Bishop's office assistant.

Ike Jameson came courting. He was thrilled when Miss Julia accepted his hand. Julia was thrilled he had straight legs and a steady job on the wharves. Her Mama got her wish, and then Ike took off his pants. That situation was not mentioned in *The Behavior Book.*

Mama told her all about what a man wants after Flossie got her curse for the first time. Johnnie Mae had been married young and knew. Cletus had been kind in courting and changed as soon as he bought that gold wedding ring. Then he used her. He used her when the drinkin' wasn't enough. This was all Johnnie Mae knew. She told her only daughter about the wifely duty, and how to stay still until the man was done. She said God gave women this burden and sometimes prayer helped in the duration. She also told her about how the sponge and vinegar might slow down the babies and how she should put it up inside her every night, just in case. She never told her daughter what might happen if you refused your man. This was something Johnnie Mae learned early never to do. Who wants another broken arm? Not her.

Julia's honeymoon night was spent in the home Ike recently made title on. She was proud to marry a man who owned a house, even if it was only one story. It had two bedrooms, a side room, and a very nice parlor. When the time came, Julia stood with her back toward him in the embroidered night dress the reverend's wife made for her. Ike very gently lifted her gown and softly kissed her shoulders. Then he saw her marks. He traced the Z with his fingertip.

"Why are you tickling me?"

"You have a scar between your shoulder blades. What happened?" Ike leaned to kiss her stripes.

The flood of fire and pain rushed in. The memory of that day when she was three struck her with horrifying force. She shivered, retched, and spun around, modesty be damned. Her movements knocked him off balance, sending him into the bedpost.

"Do not mention my back or touch me there. Do you understand? I got burned when I was little. I will not talk about it." Julia snatched her bridal finery from his hands and dropped it over her head, tears flowing. "I will lay with you, but do not speak of my body again."

Ike never asked another question about her past. After she saw his readiness, Julia followed her mother's advice and prayed the Lord's Prayer. He was finished just about at 'And deliver us from evil'. *How appropriate,* she thought.

It was the next morning, as she was removing her bridal sheets, when she noticed his penis. She had seen them on the boys back home when they went swimming in the heat of summer. Ike's was different. Then she remembered her Bible lessons. She turned her back on the bed, facing him as he dressed.

"Are you malformed?" She waved her hand in the general direction of his crotch.

"Pardon?"

"Your private thing…what's wrong with it?"

"Nothing." Ike looked down at himself. "Oh. I'm circumcised. I was born Jewish."

"Oh my heavenly Jesus," she cried. "I thought so. I am married to a Jew. You lied to me. Oh, God, oh Jesus, what am I going to do? I cannot be married to a Jew. What would the Ladies Guild say?"

Ike stared at her. "I did not lie to you." Taking a deep breath, he continued. "Besides, they will never know. They are not in our bed." He pulled on his pants and went into the kitchen where he made strong coffee and a resolution. He promised himself he would try to be the best Christian husband he could be. He pretty much succeeded.

Ike went to work the next day, leaving Julia to get to know the house on her own. He was a man of order, but didn't understand that dust undisturbed becomes mud with the humidity of the Gulf. During her first week of marriage Julia waged relentless war, polishing everything in all the rooms. She couldn't repair her husband, but she could restore his house. Besides, he was right. Nobody could see his privates. A spotless home for neighbors to visit would take care of his little problem. She was beginning to relax. She soon stopped using her sponge.

Four months into their marriage Julia missed her monthly. Maybe this situation would work out after all. The house was spotless, her parlor hosted coffee and cake parties, and she was working hard with the Women's Guild. When Julia began showing, all her friends were thrilled for her. *Yes, Mama, we did it. I am a lady.*

Chapter 5

THE BITTER TASTE OF HATE AND HOPE

"**A**hllo?"

Someone was knocking on their front screen. Julia put down her dishcloth, smoothed her apron over her bulging stomach, and walked through the parlor toward the door.

"Ahllo, is anyvone there?" A dark haired young woman with a tiny little girl was standing on the porch. They were strangers. Julia did not open the screen door. She noticed the young woman's threadbare dress.

"Yes? What do you want? You might try the Catholic Church in town for food." Julia's voice was cold and wary. The woman was foreign looking, and the little girl was practically in rags. Beggars usually did not come to front doors, and especially not women.

"I not looking for food, I looking for Isaac Jacoby. Ve were betrothed. This is his daughter, Sarah."

"Who?"

"Isaac Jacoby, my husband to be. Is he here? You tell him Esther is here to see him." The woman's voice was rising. She was looking hard at Julia.

"Madam," Julia was beginning to feel nervous. "Madam, I do not know any Isaac Jacoby. If you think someone with a name like that lives in this neighborhood, you are sadly mistaken!"

Julia reached to shut the front door. The woman stood firm. She spoke. "Ver es toig nit for zikh, toig nit for yenim. If Isaac Jacoby lives here, you tell him what Esther said," Julia stared at her. "Ve stay in this town. Ve find him sooner or later. You tell him dat, too." Julia slammed the door, locking it with a loud 'click'. Eventually they left the porch, walking slowly down the way. Whatever the woman said, it wasn't good.

That evening, after Ike hung up his hat and suit coat, Julia closed the front door and went from window to window, making sure the glass was down and the lace panels were pulled closed. Ike sat on the settee, thinking maybe tonight Julia was finally warming to his advances and would want to make time. He stretched his legs out in front of him and smiled. She turned from the last window, walked to the settee, leaned down and slapped him hard across the face. "You lying bastard, you lying son of a whore. Your bitch and her spawn were here today!"

"Whaat?" Ike was stunned. He pulled in his legs and stood up, facing his wife. "What in God's name are you talking about?"

"Your Jew woman was here with your kid. How dare you do this to me?" Julia swung at him again, this time her closed fist hit his arm.

Ike was seriously befuddled. "Jew woman, kid, what are you talking about?" He grabbed both of her wrists and held them. She started to kick, screaming curses all the while. He held her at arm's length and got his shins out of her way.

"Your bitch Esther...at our door...with a kid...for all to see. Goddam you Ike, how could you?" All that hitting and kicking was getting Julia winded. "She said...you're engaged...little girl is yours." Completely out of breath, Julia's knees buckled. Ike let go of her wrists and she crumpled to the floor, silently sobbing. He stood there in shock. The only Esther he knew was his school time chum. How in God's name did she find him way out here? They played kissing games on the stoop when they were little, but he hadn't even held her hand. Whatever this was about, the child was not his. He sat back down on the settee, waiting for her to catch her breath.

Trying to remember everything, he began. Ike told her the story of New York, of his mother and his Bubbe, and of the fast girl in school. He swore he'd never touched her except for the kissing games and he guessed she was desperate to find someone, anyone to claim the child.

"How the hell did she find you here? Oh my God, what will we do? If one person on this street saw her at our door, my reputation is ruined."

"Julia, I do not know if this is the same Esther from Brooklyn, but I do know it is not my little girl. I have no idea how she found this house nor do I care. I am sorry if you don't believe me, but it is true. My name is Ike Jameson, and that is that. He stood up. "My dear wife, clean up your language before our child is born," Ike said over his shoulder as he walked out of the room.

Julia started crying. "Oh Mama," she whispered. "Oh, Mama, forgive me. I can't be a lady if Daddy's words are still on my tongue." Sitting there on her parlor carpet, she sobbed, grieving her past life and her dear mother. When she recovered enough to stand up, she vowed. Never again would she let Cletus B. Ledbetter speak through her, no matter what.

Time brought Ike Junior. Julia had done her part by lying still and hoping for a child with sturdy stature, and if it was a boy, a natural manhood. She got both. This child would not have the marks of his father in any way, she made sure of that. Her husband's circumcision became her conscription. She kept his secret only to protect herself from society and prayed every night that the son of a bitch would die. After a while she realized not all prayers are answered.

Young Ike was raised a good Methodist, and it was such a shame that Julia could not bear any more children. In truth, Julia moved into the back room because she couldn't bear her husband. She did not believe him about that other woman, no matter what he said. Daddy hurt her, Ike hurt her. She knew never would she trust a man again.

***

"...and they saw that child do her business right

there in the yard." Julia's voice had risen with disgust. The Guild was in a full gossip when they suddenly remembered where they were.

"I am so proud of my Myra." Ada was folding work shirts on the other side of the table. She raised her head and looked directly at Julia. "Do you ladies know she has not come to us for anything since the second month after Everett died, God bless her? All she asked for was seed money to get the baking started."

Ada knew Myra was baking and selling and supporting her children. Ada also knew, with Myra's history, she'd have another belly full if she was doing anything else.

Standing in the charity room of the church, Julia listened to Ada defend her niece. Julie wrinkled her nose. Ada saw it.

"Why Julia, I know for a fact Myra sends you a sweet every day. Doesn't Mr. Jameson bring it home? She always takes him two as a thank you and another one as your gift."

Julia smiled tightly at the ladies. *That stingy bastard,* she thought. *What a son of a snake, eating the deserts she deserved for putting up with his infernal lie.* She handed the clothing packet she had been bundling to Mrs. Gaithers. Julia reached for another stack of shirts.

"I must have forgotten. Tonight I will make sure I have mine with a cup of good, strong coffee." *That's right, sister, I'll get mine.* She nodded to Ada, changed the subject, and the chatter soon lead to recipes and cooking.

As they folded, Julia began to daydream. She often would think of her sailor brother. Maybe someday there would be word of CB. She had no idea where he was or if he was even alive. All she knew was he looked like Daddy, poor soul. Julia always kept her eyes open for him when she was out and about.

She had few occasions to go to her husband's

office, but after that little bit of news about her intended sweets, she found reason often. Sometimes she saw Myra with her basket, sometimes she didn't. Not once did a plunket find its way to their dinner table. May his stingy soul rot in hell for keeping one more thing away from her.

"I saw the oddest thing today," Ike said one evening as he reached for the supper biscuit plate. The family just finished saying grace, with Young Ike offering up the 'Amen'.

"What was that, my dear?" She spread her butter, did the same for her son, but did not hand the dish to her husband.

"There was a man on the wharf who had the strangest resemblance to you. He was one of the Mates, I could tell that. He walked like one of those ugly little bull dogs, you know, with bow legs, but, by God, he could have been related to you. Do you know of any family who might be sailing?"

Julia startled at his talk, but kept her face passive. "My dear, you know I have no one left since Mama died." She never spoke of her father and allowed the assumption of his demise to be a fact. She still did not offer him the butter. "Did you watch him walk far?" What if CB was in port? How could she see him without drawing attention to herself? How could she even find him? She was surprised her heart was beating so hard.

"He walked onto the *Sallie Lousy*. That's what we call the *Sallie Lou*. She's such a dirty ship. Even their invoices stink of those spices she carries. Why do you ask?"

"Um, just making conversation." Julia thought fast. "The ladies of the Guild were talking about the results of rickets just the other day." She handed him the butter dish. "Care for jam?" She knew he did not like marmalade, so she passed that pot first.

The next day at Guild, Julia mentioned that her

husband saw a sailor with bent legs.

"What a pity for a crippled man to work so hard. I wonder if he has the rickets. Missus Ada, have you heard about oranges helping with rickets?"

"I know they help with scurvy. I thought rickets came from babyhood." Ada was considered an expert on food since her husband sold groceries.

"Wouldn't it be fine if the Guild could take oranges to the men on that ship? Prevention is worth a pound of cure." Julia ignored Ada's information about babies. "Of course we would be escorted by my husband to the gang plank. I know those men would be so grateful to come down and receive our benevolence." The room murmured in agreement. They all would go, sharing citrus and Jesus.

"You talk to the Reverend and I'll gather the board," said Ada. "The church should pay for the fruit. We do have oranges in stock."

Ada hoped if the ladies saw Myra selling her sweets, maybe they would hush-up about her and start keeping her young'uns again. Ada could only hope. Junior had been put in charge of the brood, since they were all in school. That boy was just too young, but what else could you do?

The entire Guild board was in the room. Leaving the others working at the clothing table, they quickly convened around the coffee pot, voting approval of the proposal. The idea of a forbidden adventure disguised as good deeds sounded like just the thing for proper ladies who had never even seen a sailor, let alone stepped out on a wharf. Ada volunteered to explain the sailors' plight to the Reverend. Mrs. Gaithers was asked if she would go with Ada to the store. Of course Julia said she would ask her husband to act as escort for the ladies.

When Ike told Julia that, unfortunately, he could not leave the office, she quietly vowed to spit in his supper coffee. He told her that she should know by now the importance of his job and that it required constant supervision of his staff. Ike reminded her no one could do his job except him. "He can't even make a show of caring about me for the ladies," she muttered, and decided to spit twice.

On the appointed day, every Guild member except Annie Hoffen arrived precisely on time. Mrs. Gaithers explained that, unfortunately, her sister was having trouble settling their mother this morning and knew she needed to stay in the house. Julia marched into her husband's office and was given his most junior bookkeeper as escort. Mr. Thomas, aged eighteen and living at home, had never stepped foot out of the office onto the wharves. He was almost as afraid of the ladies as he was of Mr. Jameson, but his mother told him he was a man, and he knew a man must handle challenges. He faced the ladies of the Guild and tried to smile. He led them through the office and out the back door.

The Guild followed obediently behind Mr. Thomas. Ada walked beside him, carrying the basket of oranges. The ladies blushed as the sailors whistled their way. They had no idea it wasn't them the men were noticing, it was their escort. Mr. Thomas walked to the gangplank of the *Sallie Lou,* where he stopped, completely lost as to what to do next. They all stood whispering, and looking around.

"Jumbles. Plunkets. Crybabies." The women startled to see Myra approaching them, calling her wares.

"Aunt Ada."

"Sweetheart." *Thank heavens her bonnet was straight and her apron pressed.*

"What are you and the ladies doing out here? Oh, I see Mr. Thomas is with you. Hello, Mr. Thomas. How did your mother like the jumbles you bought for her?"

Julia interrupted. "How do you do, Missus Myra?" *Grrrr, even that simple man-child took sweets home, damned Ike and his selfishness.*

"Mother really enjoyed them. She wants me to tell you thank you."

Ada held up her basket of oranges to show Myra. "Mr. Jameson told Missus Julia about the man he saw here on the docks, a man with bowed legs. The Guild wishes to give oranges to the men of his ship. You know, for the scurvy." Ada got in the last say. Julia didn't notice.

Myra smiled. "Oh. You mean Sure Foot Ledbetter."

"Dear Lord," whispered Mrs. Gaithers. "She knows their names. Heavens preserve us." Several of the ladies nodded their tight-lipped disapproval.

Julia swallowed. "Missus Myra, do you know this crippled man? We do want to make sure the gifts from our Lord go where they are needed." Ledbetter. Oh blessed God, let it be CB. She hadn't seen any family since that fateful night when she took the money and ran.

Myra laughed. "Why Missus Julia, everybody knows Sure Foot. Let me holler him down." She shifted her basket, cupped her hands around her mouth, and let out a sound that could only be described as a cat shriek. "SURE FOOT. SURE FOOT LEDBETTER. You have company. Please come down here now." The Guild tittered, Mr. Thomas shrank deep into the crowd of skirts, Ada watched, and Julia hoped, touching the letter she'd written and hidden, tucked into her left sleeve cuff.

Chapter 6

CB

CB Ledbetter was short, ugly, and smart. He hid the smart when he needed to. He knew what was expected of him and how and where to give it. When his daddy, who was just as short and ugly, but not so smart, took him to the docks and sold him, uh, err, signed him on as Deck Boy at age nine, CB knew what to do. He made sure Daddy got what was comin' to him.

CB and Cletus walked the docks that day, especially looking for a ship not fully manned, giving them the upper hand on the negotiating. Of course Cletus knew nothing about bond prices, but he did know mule trading. He figured there couldn't be much difference. They stopped at the *Sallie Lou*. She was a three-masted, steam-powered side wheeler, and after only one year, still having the new-timber smell about her. She'd been styled after the blockade runners from the War and she sure was mighty sleek.

Cletus climbed the gangplank and asked for the Captain.

"You see that fine boy down there?" The two men were standing at the deck rail. Cletus let fly a stream of chaw juice over the edge, straight at CB. "I'd be willin' to bond him for the right price. I put them muscles on him." He'd never been on a boat that moved like this one. The rocking reminded him of drinkin', and Cletus sure liked that.

Captain William J. Calhoun stepped away from the smell and squinted. "All I see is a scrawny rat. I don't see any muscles. You sure he has some?"

"Flex, boy," was yelled down to the dock. "Show them arms." CB obliged his daddy by pulling up his shirt sleeves and striking a pose. It worked.

50

The child was sold for three five dollar gold pieces, four silver and eighteen coppers. The bond was eight years, ending in 1897 when CB was seventeen. Then, if he didn't like seafaring, he could come back home. Cletus was happy with his transaction. CB was even happier. He would have paid Mr. Calhoun himself to take him away from the crazy stinkin' drunk he called Daddy. The boy's only regret was the thought of leavin' his beloved Flossie behind.

While Cletus worked the contract, CB talked to the sailors standing around. He found out where the nearest tavern was and tearfully dragged his daddy there for a good-bye whiskey.

"Oh Daddy, I'm going to miss y'all so much. I'll pour you a tot. Can I have some, too?" CB pretended to drink after his daddy. After each taste he filled the glass to the top.

"Son, I done good by, uh, fo' you. Your mama will miss ya." Cletus was beginning to slur. "I'll tell her 'bout your ship. She'll be wantin' ta know. So'll yer big sis. I'll tell 'er, too."

An hour and a bottle later Cletus was in a stupor. CB picked his daddy's pocket and cheerfully headed back to the ship. When he walked up that board to the *Sallie Lou*, he had gold, silver, and his contract in his britches. His daddy had a belly full of liquor and whatever coppers were left after the bottle. CB felt it was a fair exchange.

Cletus woke up sometime that afternoon, patted his overall leg for the coins, and headed out. It took him many miles of mule travel to realize the signed contract and the good money were gone. He was tryin' to pay for the dinner he got caught stealin' from a house by the side of the road. The owner held his shot gun at aim while Cletus dug his pockets. That's when he figured out he'd been carrying copper and nothing else all the way home.

"I'm gonna tan that boy next chance I get," he muttered to himself as he continued on with an empty belly. "That damned skunk robbed me." He told Johnnie Mae the saddest tale about being held up on the road. She knew by his smell he'd spent it on liquor. She would miss CB later on when she had time. Right now she had eleven year old Flossie to tend to.

***

Captain noticed the first day CB's bowed legs givin' him good balance as he scampered along the deck, helping the hands load. Watching this new fellow made him smile. The boy was so short. That meant he could fit into tight places. He knew the lad would do well on ship and assigned him Cabin Boy status before the first sailing. CB was soon fetching for the Captain. One day, during an especially rough sea, CB brought him his dinner tray and did not spill one drop of tea. Mr. Calhoun said, "Son, you are one sure-footed sonofabitch."

The boy shot off a sharp salute. "Yes, sir, I am."

Captain Calhoun laughed while CB snapped his suspenders and jumped in the air, clicking his heels. The name Sure Foot stuck. He liked it because no one never did tell him what CB stood for. The Cletus part, yes, but the B always left him wondering.

There was a colored Deck Boy on board just a year older than Sure Foot. The hands called him Black Jack. He had been on since first voyage. Where Sure Foot was short and fair, Black Jack was dark and tree-tall skinny. He was not bonded. His granddaddy had been a slave, and Jack Smith had been raised to respect change. So when the word got out that a new ship was taking hands, Jack ran away from his pa and the cotton. He got himself hired on the *Sallie Lou*. He felt the pull of freedom almost as strong as his granddaddy felt all those years ago.

Captain set him to teaching Sure Foot the ways of the sea. Sure Foot and Black Jack teamed up fast, worked hard, and stayed out of the way. When the hands would start on Black Jack, it was more often than not Sure Foot's clever words that would stop the ugly talk and a threat of the whip. Mr. Lincoln had done his job, but some of the sailors hadn't gotten the news yet some twenty-five years later. Sure Foot would sing a song and dance his bowlegged jig. The men would forget their what-for and watch the show. Jack would go below and hide.

One day Sure Foot followed him.

"I's sho' happy you knows the 'high step'. Thems men was gwana whup me good."

Sure Foot looked at him. He had an idea.

"Can you talk white?"

"Huh?"

"Can you talk white? You know, like me."

Jack stared at him. "Whafo?"

"What for?" Sure Foot corrected him.

"Yessuh, whafo?"

"I was thinkin' that if you didn't talk slave, the men might leave you alone."

"I's don' ta'k slave. I'h talks regler." Jack looked confused.

"You talk slave."

Jack scratched his head. He started thinkin'. He knew the itch wasn't a critter in his hair, 'cuz nigger hair couldn't hold 'em. That was one good thing. Mebe it was something else. Mebe the itch was change. Jack opened his mouth.

"Eue taaalk silllave."

"Yes, man."

"Yeeees, man."

Each time the boys had a chance Jack would practice his white talk with Sure Foot. Jack knew the benefits of being white and figured this couldn't hurt none.

They became true friends. The sailors called them Checkerboard. Sure Foot and Black Jack could sing a harmony that blended their voices to a fine sound. The words rang clear, thanks to the talking lessons. Jack learned quickly from Sure Foot, and his slave words were soon forgotten, except when needed. What Jack taught Sure Foot was something no one could ever have expected.

Captain Calhoun loved the *Sallie Lou* more than any woman he knew. He was her first love and she, his last, but just like some longstanding couples, the Captain took a mistress. His deeper love of drink caused him to ignore the *Sallie*, and that is where Sure Foot saw his opportunity.

It started with the Captain showing Sure Foot the key to the side closet. They had been to sea several weeks.

"You use this to get my liquor. I take a half glass every day at four bells."

"Yes sir. Do you drink rum or whiskey? My daddy drank new whiskey. It's a wonder he ain't blind by now."

"I enjoy brandy. You'll see it there. It's in the front."

The case was in a locked room next to the Captain's quarters. Sure Foot thought it odd the Captain had a locked room until he used the key. The room had a low ceiling and was filled with crate upon crate of all kinds of spirits. That's when Sure Foot realized his Captain was running rum on the side. There was only one opened box, and it was up front. The various liquors were arranged by labels on the crates. Even though Sure Foot couldn't read, he recognized the new whiskey with the XXX markings 'way in the back. He fetched the fancy bottle from the open crate and locked the door.

"Here you are, sir. I've never seen brandy before. Do you want me to get you a glass? How do you drink it?"

Captain Calhoun smiled. "You don't, at least not right away." He reached for a fancy flower vase that Sure Foot never noticed on the shelf. "You pour about a finger in this round thing. It's called a snifter. It's made of lead crystal. You put your nose in it and smell."

"Huh?" Sure Foot stared at his captain. "Daddy always put his whiskey in a drinkin' glass."

Captain Calhoun grimaced. "I remember your daddy. I expect he would have. Brandy is not new whiskey. Watch."

The Captain went through the ritual of pouring, cupping the snifter and swirling. When he was satisfied, he inhaled deeply from the glass.

"Ahhh. This is good. Do you want to try?"

Sure Foot had done odder things in his young life, but smelling a flower pot full of liquor was right there on top. However, he figured since it didn't kill the Captain, he would probably survive, too. Sure Foot took the snifter and breathed.

He sneezed twice.

The Captain took the brandy back and sipped. He closed his eyes, swallowed, and smiled. He spoke.

"Son, when you are old enough to drink, promise me you won't ever drink new whiskey."

"Yes, sir, I promise."

The boy never did.

Sure Foot knew Mr. Calhoun would drink what was put on his dinner tray, and if it wasn't enough, he would fetch a refill. He always poured a half glass. Sure Foot also realized that four bells, the six PM mess call, meant nothing. His captain's evening drinking started at one bell, twelve thirty PM, and continued until he slept. The boy pocketed the key his third year at sea and kept it until the end.

Chapter 7

JACK

The childbirth fever claimed his wife, leaving Abraham Lincoln Smith, first generation freed, with three sons to feed and work the fields. One day the oldest, Jack, was gone, and so was the book. Abe never knew where, but he always hoped the nine-year-old was safe. He felt, just like himself, Jack Smith was born looking for what comes next.

Young Jack knew exactly what he wanted. Being a field hand was not for him. His daddy told many a story about how the cotton got to the ocean called the Gulf. Cotton can't grow on water, so that was where he headed. What his daddy picked was baled and put on mule trains. The drivers told him the bales ended on big ships that went all over around the world. Jack packed his kit with the book, dodgers, tack, and hope. He stood by the high road, waiting.

First wagons came by. The drivers stared straight ahead. The sweaty day wore on late into the afternoon.

"You, boy, what you doin'?" This driver was white, with red hair, a stranger who met his eye. His mustache was hangin' below his cheeks.

"I's runnin' to the water. You takes me there?"

"Your mammy know?"

"She died."

"Sorry to hear. Your pappy know?"

"Yes suh," Jack lied.

"You got food?"

"Yes suh."

"Get on the back."

This driver and his men didn't mind the hitch. Five miles from the wharf, they wished him well, and Jack ended up at the *Sallie Lou*.

Captain Calhoun understood that hiring colored was wrong. A mixed ship does not sail well, everybody knew. Yet, at the end of the day, Jack Smith was given a hammock, a plate and cup, and was sent below to work bilge. Mr. Calhoun noticed the skinny boy's strong arms, and few men kept at the pumps very long, anyway. Jack stayed below for a year, out of the way, working those strong arms. The *Sallie* was dry and Jack grew tall. Sometimes the men forgot he was there, except when they heard him singing, and Lord, how the boy could sing. There seemed to be a tune echoing through the ship most of the time. The men would catch a bit of gospel or minstrel. Jack's mama sang the sweetest songs to him. She said that her mama, Granny Betty, learned all the new tunes because she was employed as a house maid for Countess Willie Piazza in New Orleans.

One day Mr. Calhoun heard some of 'Jeanie with the Light Brown Hair' floating through the wind and he headed into the hold. Jack was not aware of his captain standing there, listening. William J. Calhoun knew he had to get the boy out from below and onto the planks. Then he could hear the songs whenever he wanted. All of a sudden Jack Smith was a Deck Boy. He never knew how it happened, but he didn't stop singing.

It was just about the time when CB came aboard. Captain called him Sure Foot. Jack called him friend.

Sure Foot's daddy taught him to distrust colored, and Jack knew very few whites would take you for what you were, only seeing what they could get. So the first few months at sea when Sure Foot asked him about the book he owned, Jack didn't have much to say. Whites read, blacks don't, and he knew Sure Foot would steal it sure as you please, and he could never get it back if it was gone. The book was the only thing he owned from his mama. However, one rainy day with nothing to do, Jack finally gave in and showed it to him. He had been reading the words to the songs, trying to hum the notes.

"Show me," said Sure Foot. "Please. I won't touch it."

"Promise?"

"Promise. What's it called?"

"*The Sovereign: A Collection of Songs, Glees, Choruses, &c*" Jack said, proudly.

Jack opened to the middle. "I like this one. It's about girls."

He sang:

"I'll scream if you touch me! exclaimed a pert miss,

"Whose lover was seeking an innocent kiss.

"By this prudish conduct cold water was thrown;

"The lover drew back and left her alone.

"I'll scream if you touch me! again cried the elf:

"He said 'I'm not near you---don't trouble yourself.'

"She quickly subsided, grew tender to view,

"And whispered quite softly, 'I'll scream till you do!'"

Sure Foot'd never seen such a thing before. "You got the words from those lines and dots?"

"No," said Jack. "The lines and dots make the music. Those things below the lines make the words."

Sure Foot stared at the page. "You read? Colored don't read."

"I do."

"No kidding?"

"No kidding," Jack said with pride. "My mama taught me."

Sure Foot stared at his friend. He swallowed. "You teach me?"

"Maybe. You want learning of words or learning of music? My mama taught me both."

"Both. Can you show me?"

"Can't let the men know."

"I know."
"Can't get the book dirty."
"I know."
"I'll try."

The boys spent their next several years practicing the words and notes. They even memorized the musical catechism at the end of the book just because they could. When Mr. Calhoun found out Sure Foot could read, he was happy to have help with the charts, logs, and all kinds of paperwork. There were books in his cabin Sure Foot would ask to read. The Captain didn't mind if they were away from his shelves. He did not know that Sure Foot always gave them to Jack first, as an unspoken thank you for the learnin'. When Jack would finish the first chapter, he would retell the start and give the book to Sure Foot. Each chapter was a special share between friends. After a while they realized they were talking like the words in the book. Sure Foot would slap his leg, laughing, when Black Jack would go on like King Arthur. Sure Foot would talk a fool like Merlin, all magical and such. Together they would spin stories from the Captain's books, always ending with something about a beautiful maiden and a kiss.

Chapter 8

BEST FRIENDS AND BULLETS

The day Sure Foot shot Jack really tried their friendship. Dang, neither of them had any business hunting with a pistol. The young boys were good at sling with that new rubber strapping, and the sailors were known to lay a bet or two on their target practice. They would work their aim for hours during idle sailing days. Jack took a barrel top and painted the deadeye on it. They would prop it up against a pole and the object was to hit the center without knocking over the head. Their load was anything round and hard, but the boys liked the flat spin of a dried butter bean the best. If you tucked it into the leather thong just so, the bean would fly flat and fast. Cook didn't mind as long as they swept 'em up and got 'em back in the sack before next mess.

"Boys." Captain heard the goin's on, all the bet call and whoops, and came up out of his cabin. "Sure Foot, Jack, what are you doing? Did Cookie tell you to ruin my dinner?"

Jack grinned. "Sir, you don't especially like butter beans. I know that 'cause I've washed your plate before." He walked up to his captain.

"That's a fact, sir." Sure Foot joined him. "Do you want to give it a try? I'll set the target for you." The men standing around started to cheer. Their cap'n was always a good sport. A few wagers were made on him tippin' the target, 'cause they figured he'd never hit the eye. Most just waited to see what would happen. "Here, take my sling. Your arms are 'bout my length. Jack's got arms long as his legs." Captain Calhoun was a tad taller than Sure Foot, but not much.

"Hell, boys, I would embarrass you both. Just let me watch. I could use the entertainment." He turned to the

60

others, laughing. "I saw you put your bets. Save your money." He stood waiting, his arms folded across his massive chest. Truth was, he was a bit too pie-eyed to hit the mark and he didn't want to show it. The men knew anyway, but never said a thing within earshot of the captain. A calm ship sails smoothly, they all agreed.

After a while they added pistols to their practice. Captain remembered the runners and pirates from early days and felt his men needed to know how to shoot. Considering what happened, maybe he should have thought this out. The boys were just turning teen when they decided to go hunting agouti while docked at Panama. They'd seen them before and thought the animal was big enough to hit real easy.

"We can do it. They're just like a cat." Sure Foot was for the idea. All they had to do was sneak the guns and shot off the ship, and then actually find one of the critters and shoot it.

"Jeez, man, I didn't go to sea just to die in the jungle. How we gonna not get lost?" Jack was doubtful.

"Trust me. We ain't gonna get lost. My daddy taught me how to track." Sure Foot didn't mention he was five when the lesson occurred. "Bet we can get one. Won't the men be surprised when we come back a'swingin' that thing by its tail."

Jack looked hard at him. "You never been in a jungle, least not since I knowed you. So tell me how did your daddy teach you to track? You ain't nothin' but a farm boy. You don't even have a wild man explorin' hat."

"Can too track. Daddy took me when I was five years old. We went far out from the house into the woods and then he left me. Said we was playin' a game and not to come back. Once I got hungry, I just followed his brush break. 'Twas night by time I got home. Mama was cryin' and the house was all tore up." Sure Foot looked beyond Jack into his memories. "I think Flossie was up under the bed and Daddy was laid out on the kitchen floor, snorin'. Mama just stood there cryin', holding me to her. Don't know why." His voice trailed off. "Mebe because I lost the game? I just don't know."

Jack punched his buddy on the arm. "You're a tracker, that's for sure. All right then, let's go hunting." The memory of Jack's father came forward. Daddy Abe Smith was such a good man. *Sure Foot's daddy might be white, but that didn't make him nothin' but a dog.* Jack knew no real man would take his boy to the woods and leave him. "Let's get us some guns," said Jack. "We're goin' huntin'." The plan was set.

Each boy put a pistol in his britches and shot in his pocket. They were allowed four hours ashore after landing and unloading. The weight of the guns tucked into their waists surprised them. Shirts were out to cover the handles. Ship boys in town were often seen all loose-tailed, but Sure Foot and Jack were scared they looked somehow guilty. They walked with what they thought were man steps, chins out, long strides, scrawny boy chests puffed. Not one person paid them no never mind.

At the end of the wharf and a block into town, they realized there was no jungle, just buildings. Neither boy thought where the jungle was, just that they intended to go hunting there. Finally they walked into a cantina, forgetting they could not speak Spanish, and asked the serving man where the jungle was. The only response they got was stares and laughter. One of the men at the poker table turned and spoke.

"You hobbaadehoys better vamoose to where you come from. This ain't no place for the likes of you." He turned back to his cards after giving Jack the eye.

"We're just lookin' to go huntin'." Sure Foot knew he had to speak up. Dang, he didn't think there would be a problem with colored since this was Panama, and everyone was brown here, anyway. "You know where the jungle is?"

The boys stood taller, trying to prove they were real men.

The card player folded his hand, hit the spittoon with a strong stream of 'bacca juice, and grunted. "Damn it, quit botherin' me. Walk down this road and turn north. You'll see it soon enough. Now get the hell out of here." He turned to the table and laid down a mixed pair of aces.

Card Playin' Man was right. There stood the biggest woods either boy ever saw. Fifty paces into the growth and there was no sky. Another fifty paces and there was no trail. Jack stopped still.

"You hear that? I hear russlin'. Mebe it's agouti. Let's stand here and look." Neither boy wanted to go deeper and neither boy was going to say why. Men on wild animal hunting trips don't get scared of things that fast, so they weren't going to either. They pulled out their pistols and got them ready. Standing back to back like some kind of duel, Sure Foot whispered.

"You go that way, I'll go this. Don't step too far, don't want to lose you." Sure Foot knew trackin', but this was nothin' like he'd ever done before. However, he couldn't let on since he was the experienced one. He heard a branch snap behind him. He was gonna shoot him an agouti. He spun and fired.

"IEEEEEOW. OW. OW, OW." Jack was screaming, rolling around on the ground holding his right butt cheek. "AAAAAAH, you shot me. Jesus Almighty, you shot me in the ass." He was holding his bottom with one hand and trying to unbutton his fly with the other. "Ow, ow, ow, Jesus God, OW." He couldn't get his buttons undone, laying on his good side.

Sure Foot dropped his pistol and ran to his friend. "Oh God, oh God, oh, man, I'm sorry. I'm sorry. I'm sorry." By the time he made the few steps between them he was bawlin'. "Jesus man, let me see."

"Git away from me, you crazy sonofabitch. You shot me. I ain't no wild animal." With the frustration of trying to get his pants off, the pain and shock hit him hard. Jack was never been so angry in his life. "Damn you, Sure Foot, damn you. Why'd you shoot me?" The energy got him to his feet. With his pants half-undone and his butt bleeding, Jack Smith punched his best friend in the nose. Sure Foot heard the bone crunch from the inside out.

"Shit, you broke my nose." The two looked at each other. Jack's britches and Sure Foot's shirt were a bloody mess. A hysterical laugh hit them both.

"Lemme see yer butt." The sobs and giggles had the boys out of control. Jack dropped his pants and pulled down his drawers, giving Sure Foot a full view.

"Yep, there's a ball there. I can see it under the skin. Bleedin's done, though."

Jack was hiccupping. "Is it black like the other two?" That started the hysteria all over again. Jack pulled up his clothes. Sure Foot's nose had not decided to settle down. They stood there, Sure Foot pinching his nose, trying to stop the flow. Jack painfully bent down and picked up his loaded pistol. "Where's your gun? Can't leave it here." Sure Foot gestured with his elbow back to where he'd been standing. Jack fetched it. He disarmed his and put both in his pants.

"We gotta get fixed. Can you walk?"

"Can you? You're the one with the extra ball."

The two bloody buddies slowly made it back on ship. CB's nosebleed had stopped just about the time they hit the dock. They were heading to their hammocks after putting away the pistols when Captain Calhoun came around the edge of the hatch cover.

"Damn it, boys, you're covered with blood. You get beat up in town?"

"No sir. Jack punched me in the nose."

"Only 'cause Sure Foot shot me in the butt."

Captain Calhoun escorted them both into his quarters. After hearing their story, he rang for the cook.

Cookie used his boning knife and dug out the bullet from Jack's bottom. He used Cap'n's brandy to wash the wound and a plaster to cover the hole. Looking at Sure Foot's nose, he packed it full of lint and told him he had to sleep sitting up, for fear of drowning in his own blood. Then he left the culprits standing in front of their Captain.

"Goddamit, boys, what were you thinking? I'd tan the both of you if I thought it would do any good. You could have killed each other." He sat down at his desk, sighed, and poured himself some of the brandy used for the gunshot wound. This time he didn't sniff it. Draining his glass, he looked straight at the boys. "Go change clothes. Jack, sew that hole in your britches. Both of you get your mess and go to bed. You are confined to ship until we reach Galveston. And, for God's sake, stay away from the pistols."

Chapter 9

COMPLICATED CARGO

When Sure Foot reached his bond age in 1897, he presented his contract to Mr. Calhoun. The Captain asked him what he wanted. Since they were mid-sail to Panama, and walking on water was not one of his talents, Sure Foot decided to stay on with the *Sallie Lou*. He was a grown seventeen, with strength of any man twice his age. Mr. Calhoun knew what he had and hired him as an Ordinary Seaman. The young man negotiated the same for Black Jack. Sure Foot knew his friend had no bond, but Black Jack was not learned in mule trading. Cletus' training earned both boys a wage of eight dollars, silver, issued monthly in port. It was agreed to by all, with the stipulation they never tell the other men that both were making the same. Word couldn't get out about the *Sallie Lou* paying fair to colored.

Years passed and the neglect of *Sallie* grew. By the time his bond was up, Sure Foot had free movement of the ship. Sure Foot knew exactly how to manage the Captain since his Daddy kept the same mistress. He and Black Jack could get whatever they wanted from the sailors by rationing out the Captain's back row whiskey. Come late afternoon Mr. Calhoun would look at the charts, give Sure Foot the orders for the tiller man, and not come out of his cabin. The sailors did the best they could, but after time, the Captain's lady love became as dirty as a doxy. Sure Foot knew the *Sallie Lou's* reputation in port, but that suited him just fine, considering.

Miss Sallie, as the men called her, sailed the Gulf of Mexico. She would carry her load of travelin' men and supplies from Galveston to Panama by way of Havana. In Cuba she would pick up sugar cane and continue directly to what many men considered the gateway to the Promised

Land, the Panama Railroad. The passengers aboard left their far inland homes, wanting to get to the gold fields of the Klondike as fast as possible. They often spent their last dollar to sail to that famed land of riches. These dreamers paid a pretty penny for their passage and mining gear to be delivered to whatever other ship was waiting on the Pacific side of the Panama tracks. *Sallie Lou* would then return to Texas, stopping at Belize for mahogany. She sailed north to Frontera for the many bags of allspice berries, capsicum peppers and vanilla beans, then home to Galveston.

Early on Sure Foot noticed there were stragglers at the Galveston piers who could not make passage. There wasn't any arguing with the dock master. Fare was set with no exceptions. Black Jack and Sure Foot realized the barrels and crates belonging to the ticketed men were marked PAN/KLO and were brought aboard before the hopeful miners settled in.

"I think we can make some money." Sure Foot and Black Jack were dockside, taking a rest after loading the last of the PAN/KLO cargo. The passengers would start boarding in the morning.

Jack looked at him. "How we gwanna do that?"

"Gonna," Sure Foot corrected. "We could make some money gittin' men to the gold."

"How we 'gawna' do that?" Jack dragged the "aw" out, opening his mouth and making fish lips at his friend.

"Do you know any whores?"

Jack's eyes popped open wide.

"Ja' gonna do it? Oh no, man, don't do it. Ja' gonna get the itch." Both boys were inexperienced. Steppin' out was well discussed between the two of them, but never acted on.

"Lord, no, I ain't gonna get no itch from some hoochie gal. I got me an idea, though." Sure Foot jumped up from the barrel they were sitting on. "Do you know any whores?"

Black Jack wiggled his eyebrows and grinned. "Mebe."

Sure Foot made his way easy around town and he was aware of people noticing him. It wasn't hard, what with his bow legged appearance and all. The men in the taverns realized real quick who Sure Foot Ledbetter was with his good story to tell, and he never drank another man's whiskey. That made him welcome where ever he went. He always carried a checker board and played a mean game with his colored friend. The barmen looked forward to *Sallie Lou*'s arrival. When the game was going, the whiskey seemed to flow. The colored boy was just as quick with the story, and the drinking men never complained.

Every whore on the docks of Galveston knew what the barmen did not. The young men were doing business with them. The women were quite willing to spread the word for a few coins, and besides, those two were so nice. Neither'd ever been a customer and they both always spoke to them with true respect, just like big brothers, if you allowed that one of your brothers was colored.

With the checkerboard set up, the team went to work whenever they were in port. If Sure Foot lost three games to Jack through the night, three barrels could be filled. Those who knew the scheme would then go find the young sailors on the dock, ready to make a deal to get on ship. Gold or silver was exchanged and the hopeful travelers and their packs were put into barrels marked P/K. Once loaded, the boys would open the kegs and the stowaways would carry their gear and mix with the other travelers. No fare meant no hammock, but the boys made sure there was food. The barrels would be filled with garbage, sealed except for the bung, and rolled overboard before landing. The extra passengers would walk down the plank with the rest of the fortune seekers and all was well. Except...

The desperation in Galveston grew. Stories of the

Rush brought traveling men of means buying tickets and men of little means selling or trading their very soul for a chance at the gold. It was one of these men who offered a ruby and pearl brooch to Sure Foot after one of the evening's games.

"This was my mother's. She died ten years ago. My wife doesn't know I have it, 'though it was promised to her. Please, please take it. I have no money, but I'll be so rich when I get back. I know Millie'll forgive me when I buy her a new one." The man stared past Sure Foot. "I just know she will," he softly repeated.

Sure Foot did not understand jewelry, but he did know he'd seen fancy ladies wear such things. The exchange was made. "You go 'round back. My man will take care of you. Tell Jack you're set to go."

Shipping barrels were big. The center band was close to thirty-six inches around.

"Are you sure you're ready?" Jack was standing beside the opened conveyer of dreamers. There was a wooden box close by.

"Let's go. The gold's a waitin'." The man seemed to have forgotten his worry about his wife. The fever was in him hard.

Jack put the step box in place. "Put your gear in first and then climb in. There's room if you squat on top of your stuff."

The man looked doubtful. "You think I'll fit? My legs are pretty damned long."

"That's why you gotta squat. Once you're in and I get the top on, ya gotta brace yourself. I'm gonna tip you and roll. Keep your feet pushed hard on your gear or you'll get banged up." Black Jack closed the excited adventurer and his valise into a barrel and rolled him up the plank. Except for a few bruises and a lingering need to be sick, the new traveler was on his way.

Word got out about the funny looking hand on the

Sallie Lou. He knew his way around corners and you could work a deal with him. His colored friend would pack you up and get you on board. All you had to do was pay what you had. Soon the boys had baubles mixed in their cache of coins. However, no sailor could be seen with something they were not paid with, so the jewelry remained hidden.

Their treasures always seemed to have some coppers in them and the boys felt safe at spending them on shore. When the *Sallie Lou* was in Galveston, Sure Foot would take the coins and buy sweets from the Widow Gallaway. She was so pretty and such a good baker. All the seamen knew about her dead husband and all those babies, but Sure Foot was just happy she would talk to him while she showed him her basket. She was shorter than he was and that was a wonder. He really liked that.

"Ma'am, I have a question to ask you."

"Yes?" Myra looked straight at Sure Foot.

"What do you think of selling to colored?" He knew few ladies would take money from a black man. Missus Gallaway laughed.

"My goodness," she smiled. "That's just fine. Copper is brown, too."

Sure Foot grinned, dropped the coins in her hand and gathered up several packages of sweets to take back to Jack. As he walked up the plank, she called out, "People call me Missus Myra."

He looked over his shoulder and said, "People call me Sure Foot, Sure Foot Ledbetter." From then on, whenever the *Sallie* was in port, Sure Foot met Myra on the docks for sweets and a smile. After all, no woman ever told him her first name before.

Chapter 10

FLOSSIE

The day of the Guild's visit when Sure Foot heard his name being hollered, he looked over the deck rail at a mess of skirts. Why would Missus Myra bring him out for so many women? This he had to see.

"Missus Myra, how goes your basket?" he called.

The ladies of the Guild stood nervously waiting for the poor man to make his way down the gangplank. They knew he was bent, disfigured by the horrors of malnutrition, although the young man responding to Myra's call could hardly be described as crippled. He was homely, yes, but his bowed legs carried him with agility. He almost ran down the board, smiling broadly.

"Good to see you, Sure Foot. My basket's mighty fine and full."

"Nice to know. Who be these ladies you bring? Do they have sweet treats, too?" He tipped his cap toward the women.

Julia stepped forward. She knew she had to stop him from speaking, lest he knew her.

"My name is Missus Ike Jameson, the wife of the head gentleman in the receiving office." She stared hard at CB, willing him to not say a word. "The Methodist Women's Benevolence Guild wishes to bring you and your mates these oranges." Julia took the basket from Ada and set it on the wharf. "The fruit should help the men with the scurvy." Stepping to the side, Julia softly bumped the basket, sending some of the fruit tumbling into her skirts.

"Oh, my, I am so sorry." She quickly pulled the letter from its hiding place against her wrist and slipped it under the oranges she gathered from the spill.

CB was dumbfounded. Somewhere in his memory was his mother. This woman couldn't be her, she was far too young. This woman sounded like...Oh God, was it Flossie? What was going on? What was she doing here? He remembered that stare. His mother used it when she couldn't warn him his daddy was about to tear his behind. He looked her straight in the eye, raised one brow, said, "Thank you, ma'am," and took the basket.

"I see why they call you Sure Foot," Aunt Ada spoke up. "You appear quite capable. Do you have a Christian name?"

"Yes, ma'am. My name is CB Ledbetter. My captain calls me Sure Foot." He looked straight at Julia as he answered. She widened her eyes in response.

"Well, Mr. Ledbetter, thank you for carrying these oranges to your men." Ada smiled. "Did you plan to buy some sweets from my dear niece? She is such a good baker."

"Oh yes, ma'am." Sure Foot scrabbled in his pocket and held out four coppers. "Missus Myra, here are four brown coppers for what you wish to sell me." He knew he couldn't mention Black Jack always asked for the same thing.

"Thank you, sir," she said with extra politeness, and gave him the crybabies. "These should taste right fine with the oranges." They nodded to each other and Sure Foot turned to Julia.

"The men of the *Sallie Lou* thank you for your gift. If we cut the fruit in half, I think almost all will get a taste." His tone carried a hint of sarcasm. "We poor hungry sailors appreciate your Christian charity." There was no avoiding his words. The women looked at each other.

"Oh my, sir, we had no idea how many hands were on board. Please let us come back with more. In the meantime, I assure you the largest oranges are in the bottom of the basket. Perhaps they could be quartered." Julia gave him the stare again. The ladies behind her started to back up. They'd enjoyed their adventure to its fullest and were very ready to leave. The wharf smelled of tar and dead fish. It was far too hot to stand there much longer. How dare that man with the funny name suggest they had not done enough? Mrs. Gaithers turned on her heels and started back to the counting house, with the rest of the ladies grumbling behind her. Mr. Thomas raced after them and the Guild was in retreat. Ada kissed Myra on the cheek and followed the crowd, leaving Julia.

"Look under the oranges," she hissed through a false smile and took her departure. Sure Foot stared at the back of all those swishing skirts until Myra spoke.

"Missus Julia has a resemblance to you. You akin?"

"I have never met Ike Jameson, let alone the missus. You say she features me? Why, Missus Myra, that can't be so. I am just a homely, bent-legged sailor and she's a fine lady. What is her name?" Sure Foot and Myra watched the women as they rushed toward the office door.

"Julia, Julia Marie. I think her maiden name was Smythe." She grinned. "She works the church charity room like somebody's keeping score. My Aunt Ada says she has so much bossin' in her, Mr. Jameson must be really happy to come to work every day. That way he can, at least in there, wear the pants." She turned back toward the loading area. "You want any sweets for yourself? You tell Black Jack I appreciate his business."

Sure Foot picked out a few more crybabies. He handed over more coins, thanking her again for her treats. He gave her a wink and turned to the plank, charity basket in hand. What'd Flossie put under the oranges? He headed straight below. Once he reached his hammock, he dumped them out onto his crate. Sure enough, there was a folded piece of paper mixed with the fruit. Shaking with excitement, he opened it.

"If you can read this, you know who I am. My name is not Flossie around here. Don't find me, I will come to you. IMH"

The IMH knocked the stuffin' out of him. Mama would hug them both and say "IMH." It meant In My Heart. When Daddy was especially drunk and ugly she would gather them up, whisper IMH, and shove them behind her. They would run outside. She would then take the kissin' or the beatin', whatever was coming. She never knew which, and wasn't about to let the children see either. Those three letters brought back things best left forgotten.

Sure Foot checked the oranges. He picked the two biggest for himself and Black Jack. He took the rest, quartered them, and carried them to mess. The men looked at them, laughed, and gathered around to hear about the Christian women.

"Methodist wimmin came today to save us. Good God almighty, they were one stuck-up bunch. Missus Myra's aunty seemed the only nice one there."

"You're getting' sweet on the sweets lady." Jack couldn't help ribbing his friend.

"Shoot. I aughta change your name to Jaw Jack, you talk too much. I do think she's awful nice, though."

Sure Foot, always one for storytelling, elaborated on the truth about the women with their sour faces, expanding especially on the behavior of the clerk. The sailors all agreed that he would make some old maid a fine husband.

Sure Foot did not mention Mrs. Ike Jameson.

***

The next day Julia arrived at her husband's office with another load of fruit. She'd bought a peck of oranges herself from Harry Dickenson and carried it to the wharf.

"Julia, what are you doing here again? Can't you see I am busy?"

"Those sailors need more fruit. I'll take Mr. Thomas."

"You'd better get a move on. The *Sallie Lou*'s loading now." With a disgruntled nod toward the man, Ike

74

released Mr. Thomas as the escort. This time he wasn't so timid. When the sailors hooted, it was he who blushed... and smiled, giving a little wave of his hand. When they got to the berth of the *Sallie Lou*, Mrs. Jameson ordered him to ask for Sure Foot Ledbetter, as he was the one who took the oranges the day before.

Mr. Thomas approached a Negro hand, loading. "Boy," he said in what he thought was his strong voice. "This good lady wishes to talk to Sure Foot Ledbetter. Go fetch him now."

Black Jack stared at Mr. Thomas. "Why, yes suh, yes suh, yes suh. I's be goin' ta fetch him now. You jest wai' heah." He turned to the man beside him and said, "This bugger-boy wants Sure Foot. Might I make my leave to get him?" Both men burst into guffaws and Black Jack slowly walked up the plank, calling, "Massah Sure Foot, Massah Sure Foot. Dis heah white man wans chu." The entire loading dock howled. Mr. Thomas, not knowing what just happened, stood beside Julia, smiling. Julia stepped away, telling Mr. Thomas not to move. She knew exactly what'd transpired, but would never tell her escort. The poor child was marked and didn't even know it.

Sure Foot met Jack half way down the plank. "Why you call me down for that thing?" He pointed his finger toward the dock. He'd seen Mr. Thomas and knew why the men were laughing. Walking the rest of the way, he saw Flossie. "Why, Mrs. Jameson, what brings you here?"

"It appears the charity ladies are at it again, minus the entire flock." Black Jack answered both questions asked. "I know we will be very thankful for the fruit, won't we, men?" The men shouted their agreement. Julia realized instantly she was being mocked. She looked straight at CB.

"Might I have a word with you? Our Guild wishes only the best for the crew." She darted her eyes, indicating she wanted to get away from Mr. Thomas.

"Why, yes ma'am." CB nodded toward the escort.

"Excuse us, sir."

Leaving Mr. Thomas sputtering, CB and Flossie walked farther down the wharf. Safely away from supervision, they stood, side by side, backs to the men. Very discreetly, Flossie touched her brother's arm, her hand less than steady.

"Do you know? Is Daddy dead?"

"I have heard nothing. Sailing doesn't always have an address. What do you know?" CB's voice could barely be heard, choked to a whisper.

"Mama died. I think it was the lady disease, but I don't know for sure."

"Oh no. Anything else?"

"I have a son." Her pride was evident.

"We're sailin' tomorrow." CB leaned slightly sideways, toward her. "I will be back."

"How do I find you next time?"

"Tell Missus Myra. She's one fine woman. She can be trusted."

Standing tall, they walked back to Mr. Thomas. Sure Foot took the fruit, bid his thanks and walked the plank, holding his sister's words in his heart but not on his face. Next time.

Chapter 11

CLETUS

The Captain's books were a wonderful diversion while at sea. The boys loved to read and retell the stories to each other. These stories found their way to the taverns when CB and Jack were in the man-smuggling business. The men looking for the checker game appreciated the telling. Some knew the tales, most didn't, but all thought Sure Foot Ledbetter and his colored boy Black Jack were fine entertainment. By the end of the evening, when the hopeful travelers would count the lost games and meet up with Jack out back, Sure Foot would always have extra coins sitting by his checkerboard. He would pay the bar man for his space and pocket the rest. Later on Jack would get his split and the piddlin's went to Missus Myra's sweets. It was a satisfactory arrangement all around.

One afternoon a dirty, bow-legged drunk happened into the tavern where the checker board was set up. Sure Foot and Jack were spinnin' their tales and runnin' their game. The men who knew watched for the loss and those who didn't drank their whiskey and enjoyed the stories. The boys added some bawdy-songs to their telling, and the tavern was in high spirits. Sure Foot saw the man first. He shifted his chair around the table to hide his legs.

"That drunk's my pa," he hissed to Jack. "King me," he said out loud to interrupt the story tellin'.

"You want I tip the board and we get out?" Jack whispered.

"He won't know me grown. Just wait." Sure Foot turned his head the other direction, away from the crowd.

Cletus staggered his way to the bar. He shifted his chaw to the side of his cheek. "Whacha doin' with niggers here?" Some of his teeth were missing and the rest were stained brown.

The barman looked at the drunk. "Sir, you need a whiskey?"

"I don' drink in nigger houses."

He turned to Jack. Tobacco juice sprayed as he spoke. "Boy. Geh cher black ass outa here." Jack and Sure Foot did not move. Several of the patrons spoke up.

"Leave the boy alone. He's spinnin' stories. He ain't botherin' you."

"Yeh, what he do to you?"

Cletus reached in front of him and undid his belt. "I say, niggah, get out. I'h don' drink in nigger houses."

Sure Foot knew well what was coming next.

So did the barman. "Sir, here is your whiskey, on the house." Cletus swung back to the bar and threw down the shot. The barkeep looked straight at Jack and jerked his head toward the door, settin' down a second drink in front of Cletus. Sure Foot grabbed the board, Jack got the checkers, and they were gone. Cletus B. Ledbetter was in town, and that was not good.

No games could be lost that day. The young men hurried back to the wharf. Missus Myra was just stepping out of the counting house door on to the dock when she 'bout ran smack dab into Sure Foot.

"Oh goodness, Sure Foot, Jack. Why are you two running? See a ghost?" She smiled her pretty smile, and then realized there might be trouble on their tails. "Are you all right? What happened?"

Sure Foot remembered his talkin' to Flossie about Missus Myra, and knew this was the time. "I have to talk to you. It's important," he panted. "Not here." He looked over his shoulder at the office down the way. Mr. Jameson just might know who he was. Sure Foot felt really scared for Flossie. If Cletus were to see them and figure things out, who could tell what would happen.

"You can't be seen like you're talking to Black

Jack." Sure Foot was all flustered.

"Oh, pshaw," she said. "Don't your worry about all that. Jack," she turned directly to him. "How are you today?"

"Could be better, ma'am. You gotta listen to Sure Foot. Whatever he say, it's important." Jack nodded to her, touched his cap, and taking the checker board from Sure Foot, headed to the ship. Walking toward him was one sweet looking yella gal with long red hair in plaits. She was with her boss man and they were carrying the biggest fish he had ever seen on dock. Thinking Jack tipped his hat to her, she blushed and nodded. Jack ran up the plank with more than one thing on his mind.

Sure Foot and Myra walked slowly on down the docks, him pretending to look in her basket. "You remember when you said Missus Julia favored me?"

"Yes."

"Um, she's my sister." He rushed on. "I told her you could be trusted with this. No one must ever know. Not one soul. Do you understand?" The begging in his voice covered his usual cheerfulness.

"Yes." She stopped walking and turned to him. "Tell me. What has happened? Is she in trouble?"

"Our daddy is a really bad man. I just saw him in a tavern. He didn't notice me, I don't think. I'm scared for Flossie Mae, excuse me, Julia, 'cause she looks like mama and he might recognize her. I can take care of myself, but I cannot take care of her. He could hurt her real bad, ruin everything for her. Oh, please, Missus Myra, tell her. Warn her to stay away. Please."

"Do you think your daddy will go into town, or will he stay here on the edges?"

"He's a mean drunk. Always has been. He won't stray far from the whiskey. Will you talk to her, please? He is quick with his belt, and he might…" Sure Foot trailed off. He suddenly saw what used to happen to Mama. "Oh,

Missus Myra, keep her away from here."

"I will find her today. How long you in port?"

"Another few days."

"When you hear my call, listen for 'Sweet Cakes'. That'll mean I told her."

"Oh, Myra, thank you."

He realized he's forgotten the 'Missus' and flushed bright red. Myra reached into the basket and gave him a plunket. "You owe me," she said with a wink. Sure Foot took a deep breath and put the whole cake in his mouth. He knew he would not be anywhere in sight for a while. He wiped his mouth before he walked onboard. She headed on her way, jingling her pockets with her legs. "Crybabies, plunkets, jumbles." The rhythm of her call was disturbed by the news she carried.

That evening Myra went to the Jameson house. She knew where it was, but she'd never visited before. It was clean white, with green shutters. The front porch had painted wicker chairs and the green cushions matched. Young Ike was out front, playing marbles with some other boys. Myra stood and watched, seeing that Ikey was keen-eyed with his shooter. He looked up. "Are you Junior's mama?"

"Yes."

"You tell him he owes me a nickel."

"You tell him yourself. Is your mother home?"

"Uhuh."

Myra stepped around the boys and went up on the porch. She pulled the bell fob and heard the chime inside. Soon the door opened. Julia's face went from perfect to fearful at the sight of Myra.

"Myra, why are you here? Is Missus Ada all right? Has something happened to her?"

"I must speak with you. Can you step out?"

She grabbed her shawl hanging by the door and told her son she would be back. She never called to her husband inside. They walked down the way in silence.

"It's something else, isn't it?" Julia did not want to say too much, lest this was not about the church.

"Your brother has a message," said Myra. Julia gasped and stopped walking. "He called you Flossie. He told me your secret is to be kept, and I will. You can trust me."

"What has happened? Is he hurt? Oh dear God, please say he is safe."

"Your daddy is in town."

"No, oh no, oh no," she moaned.

"Sure Foot warns you to stay close. Don't go near the wharves and taverns. He said your daddy could end up hurting you bad. He said he's quick with the belt."

Julia felt the memories wash over her. Cletus used the belt on anyone or anything he thought crossed him. The stripes on her back suddenly ached.

"When we were little..." she gulped. "When we were little we had a pet, a hunting dog. Daddy got mad at CB and me, said we were no better than a couple of dogs. Mama stood up to him. She said we were just children doing what children do. I don't even remember if we were misbehaving." Julia started to tremble. "He hit Mama really hard. She was laying on the floor, couldn't get up. Then he turned to us. 'Don't you touch them,' she was screaming. 'Don't you worry, bitch. I ain't gonna do nothin' to your goddamn pups.'" The tears Julia had hidden for so long began. She took Myra's arm like an old friend as she walked and wept. Finally she caught her breath and went on.

"Oh, Myra, he took our coon hound outside. Then he grabbed CB and me and dragged us out, too. There was our dog, front legs tied together and hanging from the tree like a lynching. He made us watch as he used his belt to whip that dog to death. Then he lifted CB and held him up by the dog. 'Ya see, ya little bastard. That's what happens

when yer born to a bitch.' I'll never forget the sight."
Julia's sobs slowly subsided.

"Dear, you are safe with me. I will not tell a soul."
Myra patted the trembling hand on her arm. "I will let Sure
Foot know you'll stay away. He is so worried about you."

Julia pulled a handkerchief from her sleeve, blew
her nose and tidied herself. They turned back toward the
house. Julia stood up straight, all evidence of distress was
wiped from her face. She took her hand from Myra's arm
and said, "Thank you for stopping by. Let us meet again,
my dear." At the door, she ruffled Young Ike's hair, turned
to Myra and said, "I'll see you soon at the church. I am
there most afternoons. Thank you again for stopping by."
She walked into her house ramrod tall, leaving Myra with
the boys and their marbles.

"You tell your boy I want my nickel. He lost fair
and square." Young Ike sounded so serious.

Myra just looked down at the boys. *If Junior made
a bet with you, too bad, that boy has no money. Good luck
in getting nothing.* Right now nickel bets were on the
bottom of her list.

Chapter 12

PLANS AND PRESENTS

The *Sallie Lou* sailed with only three special barrels on board. Sure Foot and Black Jack did not go back to the taverns those last hours in port. On the day of departure Missus Myra walked the wharves, calling out her list of treats, and when she got by the *Sallie*, her call of 'Sweet Cakes' told of the warning given.

Sure Foot knew the next time they were in Galveston there might be danger, but at sea they were home. The only trouble there was deciding what to do with the baubles the traveling men gave them. They called them the 'unspendables'.

It was Black Jack who, again, brought up the fact that Sure Foot seemed sweet on the sweets lady.

"You should give her one of the pretty pieces. How 'bout those pearls we got?" They both laughed, knowing it would never happen.

"Shoot, man, she's fine as frog's hair, but did you notice she's still wearing her widow clothes. She has no eye for the likes of me." Sure Foot settled into the steady swish of the mop. Deck swabbin' reminded him of his mama and how she tried to keep the Texas dust at bay. Today it seemed as though the rest of the crew was assigned to rig repair and the boys moved their buckets aft to stay out of the way. Those bow legs kept him off the rigging, and that suited him fine. The men were just glad the deck duty was being done and didn't say a thing about Jack staying down.

"You could get your sister to sell them. She's a churchy." Jack knew that society ladies always seemed to have a ring or a pin or something else on them that sparkled. "She could sell them to the other women. They all like the fancies." He remembered when the bugger boy brought Missus Julia to the ship with more oranges. Sure Foot told Jack that Julia was his sister, pulling the wool over the eyes of all those church women. Flossie Mae Ledbetter had passed, just like high yellow.

"You really like Missus Myra, don't you?" Jack's dark eyes sparked with mischief. "You could buy her cakes all day long."

Sure Foot grunted, rinsed, hung up his mop, and walked away. He knew it was time to sit with the Captain and his charts. Jack turned back to his chores, chuckling at his bowlegged friend. He wished he had a pretty gal to think about. He did have one he liked looking at on the Havana wharf, but she was a whore. He knew better than to get mixed up with her. His mama had talked about the ladies of the Countess Willie Piazza house, and how they got the pox real quick. He didn't know what all that meant, but the words stayed in his head. Jack hoped someday to go courting, but he didn't know where or when. Sometimes the red haired gal he saw on the wharves with the fish man in Galveston floated through his mind, but he hadn't seen her lately. For now, he was content with his sailing, his stories and songs.

Running the route meant a lot of work at the docks, but not so much while at sea. Sure Foot served the Captain his tray and they would sit with the charts. When Mr. Calhoun was up to wanting company, he would tell the lad to bring Black Jack to his quarters. All the sailors knew the two young hands could mix a melody. The tall one sang tenor, and the short one had a fine baritone. The Captain would sip his drink and listen as the boys would make their music. The cabin door was left open and their songs would float through the ship.

Captain Calhoun had no children. Having Sure Foot and Black Jack to talk to was almost like family. In between songs, he would tell his sea faring stories. Some of them were real, some were made up from his dreams. The

Captain especially liked telling about the mermaid he fell in love with. The boys would smile and urge on his tale. His lovely lady of the sea seemed so real.

One day the Captain brought out a small mahogany box. It was slippery smooth with a deep polish. It had brass hinges and a small clasp. He gave it to Jack, him being the oldest.

"Son, do you know what this thing is?"

"A lil' treasure chest?"

"You could say that. Go ahead, open it. Take it out."

Jack had never been given a gift from the Captain. He flipped the clasp and opened the lid. It was all shiny and new, settled in the box's blue velvet lining. Jack smiled. He knew exactly what it was.

"Sir. That is one nice mouth organ."

"You know what to do with it?"

Jack looked it over, put it to his lips and blew. It squeaked real bad.

"Sir, I do not know what it is really called, but I've seen 'em before. I like the size of it." Jack measured its weight in his hand.

"If you learn to make music from it, you can keep it. If you can't, give it to your buddy. Maybe he can make it blow. Either way, don't give it back."

"Yes sir, thank you sir." Jack tried again, this time not so hard. A true note came out. Jack's eyes went wide, and the Captain smiled.

"Well, boy, you just might get this thing to work. It's called a harmonica."

"Let me try." Sure Foot was not one to let something slide. Jack handed it over. The Captain grinned. Sure Foot wiped the harmonica on his sleeve and put it to his mouth. He sucked air and the thing wheezed. Everybody laughed. He wiped it again and gave it back to Jack.

"I'll learn it after you."

Jack knew there'd be more lessons coming between them, but first he'd have to teach himself. After that, Black Jack spent many an hour honkin' and squawkin' on that thing. Slowly the notes started coming easier and easier. One day he realized the music was there and he played for the Captain. Mr. Calhoun sat with tears in his eyes as Jack played 'Softly and Tenderly Jesus Is Calling'. Sure Foot joined in the chorus with:

"Come home, come home,

"You who are weary, come home;

"Earnestly, tenderly, Jesus is calling,

"Calling, O sinner, come home!"

Mr. Calhoun wiped his eyes, thanked the two and sent them on their way. He then very quietly poured another glass, lifted it in a tearful toast, and spoke.

"My dearest darling, I salute you. I wish you well." Many years ago his sweetheart left him for another, a man who would always be at home. The Captain's love of the sea and whiskey had taken her place. This song reminded him of the times he would stand beside her, sharing the hymnal in church. She now lived in Austin, last time he heard. He hoped that she found what she wanted on her ranch with all those acres of land. William J. Calhoun found his peace with the rocking of the waves. The girl's name was Sallie Lou. Her memory became his mermaid.

Chapter 13

THE BROOKLYN BRIDGE

Ike didn't recognize her at first. He was far too interested in his eggs, ham biscuits, and black coffee to pay attention to the breakfast crowd. He always sat at the same corner table so he could spread out the Galveston News without bothering anybody. This early morning time alone became a ritual Ike enjoyed immensely.

"I see you eat ham." The woman was standing beside the table. Her hat was hung down her back, country style, showing wavy brown hair. Her dress was clean but worn, and some of her buttons were replaced. "Ven did you start that? Your Bubbe vould not like."

"Pardon me?" Who was this woman? Why did she mention his breakfast menu? And his grandmother?

"Ham." She pointed at his biscuit. "You ver always a rebel." Then she smiled the slightest smile. "You don't remember me, do you?"

He stared at her, hearing words spoken from his childhood. "Are you Esther from Brooklyn?"

"Yes, and you are Isaac from Brooklyn. May I sit down?" He nodded. Susanna, his favorite waitress, brought another mug and the coffee pot.

"Ma'am?" Esther nodded and the steaming cup was filled in front of her. "Breakfast?" Susanna stood by, waiting.

"Just toast bread, no ham, thank you."

Ike recovered enough to nod to the waitress, dismissing her. Turning to Esther, he took a deep breath. "How in the world did you find me? After all, it is a bit of a stretch from New York to Texas. I never told anyone where I ended up. How did you know?" His hands were clenching under the table, grabbing at his trousers. *Abishter*, he wanted to hug her. If only he could talk about the old neighborhood, find out what happened to his family. He kept a tight hold of his pant legs and smiled.

"I saw you many years ago, ven Sarah and I first came here. I followed you one day and found your house. I vatched until I vas sure. I vanted to talk to you."

"Oh, it was you." Ike remembered Julia's rage. She moved out of the bedroom that night. His smile disappeared. "Damn it, woman, you told my wife we were engaged and your girl was my child." Ike was holding his rising anger in his clenched hands. "Were you crazy? You and I never, uh uh, never. We were kids. Why in God's name did you say I was the child's father?" Fists still under the table, Ike was beginning to show his feelings. His body reddened and his shoulders started to vibrate.

"Ma'am, here is your breakfast. Sure you don't want meat? Ike, here's your jam." Susanna noticed the coffee was untouched. "Want anything more? Just holler."

A very quiet tear spilled from Esther's left eye. "I know you're not her Papa. Back then, ven I first come here, I vas running away. I was so surprised to see somevon from home. I didn't know you ver married." Esther's tears were glistening. "Ven that voman came to the door, and the vay she act to me, I velt shame. All I vanted vas to talk vith you. She vas so mean to me. She treated me like a begger." Esther's cheeks were wet. She dabbed her face with her napkin, sniffled, and picked up her mug. The coffee was lukewarm but she sipped it, anyway. "My Sarah's papa is dead before she vas born. Ve vere *sidduch*, with the marriage day the next week. I vas in love. He vas killed by a robber. That made no sense, him being so poor. Anyvay, I stayed until my beloved *eyfel* vas born and then ve left. There was so much talk. Ve traveled a long time and lived many places. When I saw you one day, I only hoped you vould remember me. You vern't there at the house." She took a small bite of her breakfast.

Ike unclenched his hands and stretched out his

fingers under the table. Reaching for his coffee, he grimaced at the taste. "Susanna, any hot brew over there?" Two new steaming mugs arrived with another pot of jam. "Honey?" she asked. Esther smiled and nodded. As she took another bite of the sweetened toast, Ike noticed for the first time she wore a thin wedding ring. "You're married. That's good. What is your name?"

"I am Mrs. Esther Cohen, wife of Rabbi Joseph Cohen. Ve met at temple. Ve live close by. My Joe is a good man. He give Sarah his name. Do you have child?"

"My son is named after me. He is Ike Jameson, Jr." He did not look at her as he spoke.

"I see," was all she said.

Ike cleared his throat. "I've got to get going, but I am glad you saw me this morning. I would like for us to talk. I have always wondered about the old neighborhood, my mother. I eat breakfast here every day except Sunday. Maybe I will see you again. For now, please excuse me. Work waits for no man." He stood up, put some money on table and picked up his newspaper. Nodding toward Esther, he walked to the door. Susanna watched him leave and then approached the table. "He's a nice man."

"Oh? Ver es toig nit for zikh, toig nit for yenim." Esther stood.

"What does that mean? I know it's not English," Susanna asked. By the woman's tone she could tell the words were not a compliment.

Esther walked slowly toward the exit. Turning back to the waitress, she said, "He who is no good to himself is not good to another." She wondered if she would ever see him again. Probably not.

Chapter 14

OPERATION JB

It was about this time that Benjy figured out how to bring out the worst in the whole situation. While Junior was bossin' the children, Benjy was turning into a little crook. He was clever and quick. The neighborhood was beginning to notice things here and there. Back doors were always open and Benjy was hittin' the cookie jars. It seems his mama never ended up with any leftovers since she was such a good seller. Mrs. Johnson's was his favorite. Her jam thumbprints called out his name on a regular basis. Neighbor women were heard falsely accusing their own children of theft. Soon spoons and pies were gone. Benjy would head out back behind the garden, eat the whole thing, return the empty pan and keep the spoon as a souvenir. Myra was too tired to notice the boy's dinner appetite and Junior was learning it was easier not to miss him during the day because of havin' to watch the little ones.

One day Benjy decided to try his luck at lifting more than spoons. Uncle Harry's store was just the place, he thought. He was loved with all the hearts there and knew he could nick penny candy with no problem what-so-ever. When Sulee caught him suckin' on a root beer ball, she thought Harry had given it. What she didn't know was that Harry had seen the whole thing and decided to bide his time. Sure enough, the boy did it again, next time he came in. Harry watched closer and then went upstairs.

St. James Lodge No. 3 A.F. & A.M. was situated in the entire second story of the grocery building and Harry was Past Master. When the Brothers weren't in the business of being Masons, the lodge kitchen was used for wife dodging. There was always a Brother or two sitting in the kitchen, drinking coffee.

"Afternoon, Brother Elmer."

"Brother Harry."

"Have you seen Brother Turner around?"

"Not recently. You got someone to catch?" Brother Robearde Turner was the local constable, and he prided himself in running a tight district.

"Not one to catch, just one to scare." Harry poured himself a cup, sat down at the table and told Brother Elmer about Benjy. "That boy's been in my candy case. Thinks stealin's easy. Here's what I have in mind."

After a discussion on the subject, the gentlemen agreed that Harry's plan was solid. Their handshake sealed the story and Harry went back down to work. That night after lodge, he went to The Shoe. Myra was all for 'JB', the plan's name. Then they waited.

Two days later Benjy was back at the store, this time nosing around the till box. It was kept behind the counter, out of the way on a lower shelf. There were no customers so Harry and Sulee went to tend to some stock crates in the back. Sulee went out the back door and ran to the Constabulary as fast as she could. Looking both ways to make sure he was alone, the boy slowly lifted the lid. The coins were shiny and the stack of bills was high. Money sure was better than candy. He reached, snatched a dollar, and was crumpling it into a ball when a whistle blew.

"Freeze thief."

Constable Turner stood in the front door, whistle in one hand and Billy club in the other. Benjy shoved the dollar in his coveralls pocket and stuck out his chin. No one could boss him 'cept his mama.

"I saw that." He nodded at the returning Harry. "I'm cuffin' this thief. You object?"

"Not one bit. Jail him."

Benjy just stared at his Uncle Harry. What was going on?

"You take him and keep him. I'll tell his mother he

won't be coming home for a long time." Uncle Harry went straight for the lump in Benjy's pocket. "I'll just put my money back."

"No sir, the money is evidence. Give it to me, it's for the judge." Harry handed him the dollar. Benjy's chin started trembling. "Damn it, boy. Don't you go blubbering up. The drunks in the cell don't like to be disturbed." The two brothers palmed off the dollar with a Masonic shake. Constable Turner grabbed the back of the boy's coverall straps and practically lifted him off the floor. "Come on, you little turd pile. Let's find a cell that's not too crowded." As soon as the child was dragged out the door, Harry followed and ran upstairs. Almost all the men not working were sitting in the kitchen, wearing their worst clothes, and talking. Harry got what he needed.

After taking the long way through town, Constable Turner shoved the boy through the jailhouse door. Taking out a huge ring of keys, he sorted through them until he found the one he wanted.

"We don't have no holding cell for someone young as you," he said to Benjy. "You'll go to chain gang later, but for now, you get the drunk tank. Judge will probably see you sometime this week or next."

Drunk tank? Chain gang? Judge? What would his mama say? That's when the crying started.

"I told you the drunks don't like being disturbed. It gets 'em riled up. Suck up those tears, before they wipe your face for you." The constable unlocked the door and strong-armed the boy into the biggest cell in the jail. It was filled with old, smelly men. With a clang the bars were shut. The boy squared his shoulders and pushed his too-long black hair out of his eyes. He shoved his fists in his pockets and stared defiantly ahead. Drunks were everywhere.

"You's in for drinkin', too?" A very tall, dirty man in a funny looking little hat swayed toward him. "You's got

anything in your pockets? We sure'd like some hooch."
The drunk stood over top Benjy and reached for his bib
pocket. Benjy yanked his hands up to ward off the man. He
ducked and ran around him, only to bump into another. He
was as wide as he was tall and smiled funny, showing black
teeth. The man sniffed. Benjy tried to hide behind him.

"Dang it, Joe, can't you see he's sober. I don' smell
nothin' on him," said the fat man. "I bet he's in for horse
thievin'." He turned to the boy who was trying his best to
become invisible. "You been horse thievin'? That'll get
you five years on the chain gang, absolute certain. You
ain't goin' home to yer Mama until 1903. Sure am glad I'm
not in your shoes."

The rest of the drunks circled 'round him. They
were all betting on what he had done. Horse thief, whore
mongering, and bank robbing were the top three choices.
Benjy finally spoke up.

"I, I, uh, stole from my uncle's cash box."

All the men opened their eyes wide and started
backing away from the boy. There was a slow rumble
sounding among them. They pushed themselves up against
the back walls of the cell. An old bearded man stayed to the
front. He went to the door and started hollering.

"Jailer, git us out of here. This boy's too much for
us men. We done nothin' but drink. This piece of dirt
robbed family. Git us away from him." The bearded man
turned, spit on the floor, and joined the others around the
edges. They all stood staring. Benjy was shaking so hard he
feared he couldn't stay standing. This time he didn't stop
his boo-hoo. The sobs came hard and fast. Constable
Turner came around the corner, opened the gate, and led
the men out, not looking back at the boy. The last man out
slammed the gate and they all disappeared. When the
officer returned, he stood outside and tapped his Billy club
on the bars.

"Boy, what is your mama going to think when she

has to visit you? Tell me about your twin? Is he going to want to be like you? You're ruinin' your family name." The constable continued to tap. "Your Uncle Harry is one fine man. You have hurt him and your Aunt Ada bad. What about your daddy? I bet he's turnin' in his grave. If you have stolen anything else, you had better come clean." With that, Brother Robearde Turner put his club away, opened the cell and walked straight to the hysterical child. He stood there and waited.

Finally Benjy stopped shaking and crying. The man handed the eight year old boy his handkerchief to mop his face and sat down on a side bench, putting the child in front of him, eye level. Sniffling and snotting, the boy told everything. He told about how he figured how to get away from Junior and go in people's houses. He told about the cookies. Then he told about the pies, and even where he had hid the spoons. By the time the child confessed the candy and the dollar, he was blubbering again. His shame was beyond control. That's when Uncle Harry and his mother came into the jail. His mother opened the barred door, walked into the cage holding her son, and stood, arms stiff at her side.

"Oh Mama, I am so sorry." He ran to her, arms outstretched. She did not embrace him.

"Son, you have caused much trouble. Face your uncle." Myra took his quaking shoulders and turned him. "Tell your uncle what you must." Benjy stared at the floor. Myra swatted a hard one on his bottom. "Face your uncle." The boy slowly lifted his head.

"Uncle Harry, I have robbed you. The men called me dirt. I gotta make things right 'tween us before I go to the chain gang." The tears were pouring off his chin. "The men talked about five years. Oh, Uncle Harry, I am so ashamed."

"Use your handkerchief, boy."

"Please, please forgive me. I will never steal again."

He swabbed his face and blew his nose. "Oh Mama, will you remember me in five years?" Constable Turner stepped back and pulled out the Masonic Bible he had hidden inside his shirt. He held it flat on his palm, cover up. With a soft nod to the adults, he addressed the boy.

"This here is the sacred Book. Do you swear to go straight from now on?" The child nodded. "Put your left hand on the symbol of the Square and Compass and raise your right." Benjy shoved the handkerchief in his pocket and did as he was told. "Repeat after me. I, Benjamin Gallaway, swear to never commit a crime or bring shame to my family again. I will apologize to my family and neighbors and return all the spoons. So help me God."

After the tearful oath, his mother took him in the tightest hold and rocked him until they were both breathing normally. All were escorted to the door of the jail house. Uncle Harry told Benjy to shake Constable Turner's hand, and then the Brothers did the same. It was late of the evening before the spoons were all sorted and returned to their rightful households, with Benjy begging forgiveness at each door. The next day the boy realized he truly wasn't going to the chain gang. He knew Mr. Turner was one fine man.

Uncle Harry went straight upstairs when he got back from the jail. The men were waiting, drinking coffee and eating the lemon cream cake Ada left on the steps. The Brothers were enjoying the telling of what they had done.

Everyone knew Rabbi Cohen was a tea drinker and he was well complemented on his drunk acting. Robearde beat Harry to the lodge kitchen and told them all about the swearing. Harry cut himself a slice, poured a cup, and joined in. The Masons had done their good deed for the day. They all agreed. Operation Jail Bird was a roaring success.

Chapter 15

IN MY HEART

As with all scandals, the news about the jailing of Benjy was soon in the houses of the Masons and out on the docks. The women harrumphed and clucked, the men joked, and the sailors bought more sweets. The story of poor Widow Gallaway with her ne'er-do-well child-turned-good did more to cement Myra's acceptance on the wharves than anything else so far.

"My Benjy sure got his gizzard shook the other day. Thank Heavens for those jailed Masons." The lead of 'gizzard shook' and 'jailed Masons' brought the attention of the sailors from each newly berthed ship. Once they heard the story of 'bad boy redeemed', they freely spent their coins. Business boomed. It was during this time that the *Sallie Lou* came back into port. Myra was becoming fond of her chats with Sure Foot, and was very happy to see the *Sallie*.

"Oh sailor man, oh sailor man," she sang.

Jack heard the call first and helped spread the word throughout the ship. His pure tenor mimicked her alto. "Fine things are in her basket." Captain stopped him in the passage.

"Ask Sure Foot to fetch me some crybabies."

"Yes sir."

By the time Sure Foot got down off deck with the Captain's request, Myra was surrounded by the hungry sailors. He spoke up from behind the crowd.

"Captain wants crybabies."

Myra was mid story about the Masons. "Those good men made him swear on the Bible." Her head jerked at the sound 'crybabies' and she smiled at the sight of her blond friend. "Why, Mister Sure Foot Ledbetter, what's that you say about your Captain? He wants crybabies?

Excuse me, gentlemen, let me serve your Captain." The sailors made passage for Sure Foot. The look on Myra's face said more than wanting to serve the captain. It said 'Well, hello there.' The bowlegged sailor met her smile with his own. That exchange got him ribbed for the next several days. He didn't mind. "Missus Myra, do you have sweet cakes?"

Myra startled. 'Sweet cakes' was the signal for his sister.

"What flavor sweet cakes?"

"Oh, the best kind, the kind you would take home to family."

Myra turned to the sailors standing about. "Gentlemen, let me show this Captain's man my best sweets. Please come back another time." The sailors nudged each other and called rude things out to Sure Foot as they stepped away. They would love to have a taste of her 'best sweets'. Myra looked straight at Sure Foot as he fidgeted through her basket. When the dock was cleared, he spoke.

"Please tell Flossie, er, Julia that I wish she would come by the counting house sometime soon so I can see her. The *Sallie* sails in five days. I want her to know we are family and we must stick together." Sure Foot cleared his throat. "I've missed her so much."

Myra wrinkled her eyebrow. "What about your daddy? Is Julia safe?"

"I don't know," said Sure Foot. "Have you seen anyone who looks like me only mean?"

"No. Maybe he's gone away."

"I hope. Please tell her to be very careful. I really want to see her, and…that she's in my heart."

Myra pulled out a packet of six cyrbabies and another of mixed goods. "You and Jack split out this one. I'll find Julia after supper." Loudly she said, "Is that all for your Captain? Tell him ten cents. I'll collect tomorrow."

With another smile she stepped on down the way, calling her song.

The basket emptied quickly and Myra was free by mid-afternoon. She decided to stop by the church perchance Julia might be in the guild room. She knew Aunt Ada would be working the food parcels. She long ago turned the charity pantry into her own little grocery store. If there was one thing that woman could do, it was organize. Today the dry closet seemed to have been invaded by a family of mice who decided to invite their second cousins and all their unnamed children to the feast. Several loaves of bread had seen a better day. Ada was not fit for proper conversation as she cleaned up the crumbs, muttering her husband's lesser language under her breath. Myra stood at the door, smiling to herself. She loved her Aunt Ada so much.

"Auntie, do you want some help? I know how to sweep and swear, too." The women looked each other in the eye and burst into laughter.

"Thank you, darling, but no. I want to do all the cussing myself. What brings you here so early in the afternoon?"

"Basket's empty. I thought I'd come by for a bit. Who's in today?"

"I saw Miss Annie and Julia in the choir room. Good to see Miss Annie get out of the house for an hour. She was smiling. I'm sure Julia has everything in control, including Miss Annie, bless her heart. Why don't you go say hello?"

With a quick cheek-peck, Myra made her way down the hall and up the steps to the choir room. It was situated in a tomb-like tower three stories above the chancel behind the organ pipes. When the first chords of the Gathering Song were struck, the choir would make their way down to the loft and file in with the solemnity of a funeral. The sounding pipes resonated so much in the music room.

Anyone there during the time of services or practices would be deafened. Tending to the room could only happen mid-week. Once a month the robes would be hauled down and aired out in the inner courtyard. Texas heat, fine clothing, and heavy robes meant odors the Sunday morning flowers couldn't cover. The women would string ropes on hooks and hang the robes for the freshening. While the breeze took care of the robes, the choir committee would dust the room and organize the music.

As Myra was heading to the open door from the loft up to the steps behind the pipes, Miss Annie was hurrying down. The women nodded as they passed.

"Time for Mother's tonic," Annie said with an unusually bright smile.

Myra watched the back of the departing woman. Julia slowly followed, shaking her head.

"What's Miss Annie's rush?" asked Myra.

"And a proper hello to you." Julia had a way of finding fault with the least things.

Today Myra didn't fall for her ways. She looked behind her to make sure Miss Annie was gone. "Sure Foot says he wants you to please come to the counting house soon because they sail in five days."

"Did he say why?"

"No. He said for me to tell you that 'We are family' and that you are in his heart." Myra took a breath. "His Captain owes me for his cakes and I will see Sure Foot tomorrow to collect. Do you want to bring more oranges and walk with me?"

So an unlikely alliance was born. They agreed to meet near the counting house at nine AM. If they walked in together, Mr. Jameson wouldn't have to provide that poor simp Mr. Thomas as escort. The women knew they did not need his gossipy nose stuck into anything to do with this. The women separated on the church front steps, one walking uptown and one walking down. Julia stopped for oranges on the way home.

***

The next morning Julia did not tell Ike about her plans for the day. Standing on her front porch at six thirty, she kissed her son goodbye as he left for school. Lessons started at seven, and she couldn't let him be late. She loved seeing him off, admiring his strong, straight legs. Never for a moment did she take for granted even that could have gone so terribly wrong, thank God. Her husband left an hour ago. His habit was to take his first meal at Ben's Breakfast and Beef down by the wharf. There he could get as much butter and peach jam as he wanted on his biscuits, no problem. The couple was satisfied with the arrangement, especially Ike, who hoped to someday see Esther again.

As soon as her son was out of sight, Julia went to the back store room and loaded oranges from the crate box into her best tote. It held half the count she took before. That way she would have to come again tomorrow. She arrived at the lead to the wharf with a time to spare. It was her first time there since the warning about her father and she kept a wary eye open. Her excitement was bubbling, but Julia worked at keeping it still. She hid another message below the fruit just like before. Myra rushed up to her a few minutes later with her long brown hair blowing loose beneath her bonnet.

"Sorry I'm late," gasped Myra. "I hate the widow's weeds, but they sell cakes. Let me pin up my hair." Without asking, she handed Julia her basket so she could finish her grooming. "I didn't get this morning's baking done early enough and Nora Lee decided to pitch a cat-fit. It took the twins to chase her and me to dress her. I'm not sure, but I think her petticoat is on inside-out. I should have used a switch, but I didn't want to be late. Remind me to do it later." She re-tied her bonnet and took back her still warm livelihood. "Am I straight?" she asked Julia.

Julia just stared at her. She was aghast on so many

counts and, my goodness, that basket was heavy. She thanked God she had a husband who supported her, did not give her any more children, and handled their son. This was the first time in a long time she allowed a kind thought about Ike Jameson. She decided to take the marmalade off the table. That should be reward enough.

"Tighten your bow."

Myra walked into the counting house ahead of Julia. Whenever Myra entered, the room would light up and the men knew that they would make their purchases later. She would quietly put the required treats on Ike's desk and make her way out the back. When Ike saw Julia coming in behind, he knew his claim to all the sweets was over. He rushed up to her.

"Dear, what brings you here? It has been a while." He tried to walk between her and his desk where Myra had put his package. He turned himself sideways, trying to make a bigger block. "What is in your tote?"

Julia attempted to smile. It was feeble. "Oranges. Missus Myra is escorting me for my charity work. You won't have to release Mr. Thomas. I am sure you appreciate not losing man hours on my account." She gave up the attempt. "Myra and I will be on our way." She took the other woman's arm and they walked out the back door as bold as buttons and onto the wharf. Ike just stared. What would the dock master have to say about his wife walking without a man? He only hoped that Myra would do.

Once outside the door, Myra started her calling. "Jumbles, Plunkets, Crybabies," The sailors brought their coins and business was brisk. Julia stood to the back and watched. Myra sure knew how to sell. However, when they got to the *Sallie Lou*, Myra's call changed to 'sweet cakes'. Sure Foot was down the plank like it had been hog-fat greased. He held the Captain's money and hoped within hope Myra had news of Flossie. When he saw both women were there, he felt his heart stand still. It was that moment he knew.

Chapter 16

BIBLE LESSONS

"**M**issus Myra, Missus Jameson, how do you both do?" Sure Foot touched his cap. Julia lowered her eyes toward her tote. She felt that if she actually looked at her brother, she would be crying in his arms. Myra saved the moment.

"Missus Jameson brought more fruit from the church. Did you bring me my money from yesterday?"

"Yes ma'am." He held out the Captain's ten cents and turned to Flossie. "Thank you for coming and bringing the oranges. We sailors always need good things. Any messages for our souls from the good women of your congregation?"

"You are welcome. Yes there is." Julia gave him the Mama look. "Words for the soul are words worth reading."

Taking the sack, Sure Foot weighed the offering. "Looks like we will be splittin' the fruit again. I will take this to my hammock."

"Yes, I know. There is more fruit at my house. If you would empty this carry-all, I will return tomorrow with the rest." Flossie's mama eyes were boring straight through him. "Missus Myra said we could retrieve the sack as we pass by on the way home."

With a nod and a tip of the cap, Sure Foot ran up the gang plank almost as fast as he came down. Myra started her singsong and the women made their way down the wharf.

"He was always moving when he was a boy. Those legs never slowed him down." Julia smiled to herself. "I remember when he was a teeny one. He didn't learn to walk, he learned to run. Mama kept him strapped to her like an Indian just so he wouldn't get into things." *I am so lucky Ike Junior is straight-legged*, she thought to herself. Then she told Myra about her plan.

***

Once at his hammock, Sure Foot dumped the sack. Sure enough, there was a note. He read it twice.

'I know how we can see each other. IMH'

He shoved the empty tote under his shirt, put the note in his pocket, and went about his duties. As soon as he heard 'sweet cakes', he was back down on the dock. It was obvious the women were full of plans, as there was more than a little sparkle in their eyes.

"Pennies for crybabies? Yes sir. Tell Mr. Jack 'thank you'. By the way, my friend here, Missus Jameson, would like to offer you a chance to learn the wisdom of Jesus Christ." Myra's winking and eyebrow wiggling wouldn't have fooled a soul standin' by. Thank Heavens there weren't any.

Julia chimed in. "Bible study is tomorrow, two PM at the First Methodist Church. Come by the back."

Sure Foot couldn't imagine himself studying a Bible, but if this was a way to see Flossie, he would do it.

"Yes, ma'am. I'll be there." His eyebrows were doing a dance of their own. "Missus Myra, will you be in on the lessons?"

"Only if you want all five young'uns learnin' with us." She laughed. "Then you'd hear Bible words for sure. No thank you. Missus Julia can do the teachin' just fine." She took a step away from the two. CB handed the empty bag to his sister. He touched his chest and extended his hand as a good bye gesture. Julia followed suit, and walked after Myra. Before they entered the back door of the counting house, she grabbed Myra's hand and gave it a squeeze. "Thank you, dear."

She entered the office with her face wiped blank and her head up a notch too high. With a glare that could cut ice, Julia led Myra through as though she owned the place. At the door she turned and said, "Aren't Missus

Myra's deserts delicious? I know I will enjoy mine tonight, won't I, husband dear?" Julia walked out the door. Myra smiled. Now was the time to sell to the office men. As usual, she left with an empty basket and full pockets. She loved the sound. It meant supper for her family.

"Hmmm, that Julia sure is smart," Myra mused to herself as she walked home. "I can't imagine being in the pickle she's in." She chuckled. "I couldn't pretend to be someone else if I tried. I have too many young'uns callin' me Mama, bless their hearts."

The boys did not share the oranges with their mates. Their juicy feast was held later during the afternoon in the back kitchen of the *Fat*, with Clarisse and Maude getting a cut. After some time, Maude went out front while Clarisse went to the outer shed to get dried rags for the bar. The boys were expecting to work. The harmonica, the singing, the checkers…all were part of the evening's plan. Knowing the room was empty, Sure Foot told Jack about the tomorrow's Bible lessons. "Man, if it gets me a chance to talk alone with her, I'll learn Latin. Then you can call me Pope."

Jack sat very still and stared at his best friend. "Do you remember what we talked about concerning the unspendables?"

"What?"

"That your sister was a church lady. Do you think she's too high falutin' to help us?"

"Hell, I don't know, but I tell you this. I got nothin' to lose. If I don't talk to her tomorrow, I probably never will." With that said, they washed their hands, getting ready to go out front to do business. Just then Clarisse swung in the back door, leaving the screen open. Behind her was a light skinned colored girl with a basket of oysters.

"You wait here. I'll ask Maude if he wants to make stew tonight." The girl looked up into the room and blushed, recognizing Jack. After all, not many men had ever tipped their hat to her. Mostly they turned away because of her skin and her reddish hair.

"Comment ca va?"

Jack startled. She talked like his mama.

"Ca va bien." He didn't know much Louisiana talk, but he did recall the response for 'How are you?' It was the fish gal from the docks, the one with the red hair. She smiled. Jack noticed she had good teeth. He smiled back.

"Parlez-vous Anglais?" He could only hope because he used up all of his French already.

"Yes." Her cheeks almost matched her hair.

"My name is Jack Smith."

"My name is Marguerite Black."

"Pleased to meet you."

"Same."

The introductions were interrupted by Clarisse returning to buy the entire lot of oysters. Marguerite took the money, emptied the basket on the sink sideboard, made a small curtsy, and turned to leave. Jack spoke up.

"I'll look for you on the wharves, if that's all right. Maybe you could teach me some more French?" She made a small nod and left. *Humph, there just might could be more than stew in my future,* Jack thought, with a slight smile.

Two games were lost that night. By chance, one of the new passengers paid with a yellow diamond ring and a beautifully carved cameo broach. There was no way in the world the boys could exchange those. It looked like fate was steppin' in.

Chapter 17

COFFEE POT BLUES

When the church bell rang two, CB Ledbetter was standing by the back kitchen entrance of the First Methodist Church. He felt like running, he felt like singing. He knew he didn't belong in any Bible study, but, damn, he wanted a visit with Flossie. The runnin' decision almost won out when the door opened a crack and she was there.

"Shhhh." Flossie put her finger to her lips and gestured with her head. Following her eyes, he saw an attached storage shed a few yards from where they stood. She jerked her chin sideways. Oh, she wanted him to go in the lean-to. He smiled and nodded. She shut the kitchen door.

His sister was waiting for him inside, by an access door on the far side of the shed. She ran to his arms, sobbing silently. His own tears dampened her sleeve. They held on for what seemed forever. Then he stepped back from her.

"You really don't plan to teach me Bible in a storage bin, do you?"

"I don't plan to teach you a thing, but you have to admit you're here." She started chuckling. "Oh, CB, isn't this the best place to meet? I even carried out chairs from the Sunday School room." CB noticed they were not in the dark. "I brought a lantern and a table to put it on. See, we have a parlor. The back door leads to the social hall pantry, and no one ever uses it except when there's a wedding. That's how they bring in the cake." She giggled. She sounded like the little girl he used to torment and try to protect. He sat down and they began to talk.

Flossie listened to the tales of high seas. CB talked about music and how the colored hand Jack taught him to read. Flossie didn't know any colored who could read, and was very impressed. She told him about her lady lessons from Mama and how she had made her way to Galveston by assisting school teachers with the unruly students. A few detentions with the new helper, Miss Smythe, was all that was needed to set the hooligans straight. Then she would be on her way.

"The only thing I could think about was getting as far away from Daddy as I could and maybe finding you. I never thought I would see you again. I just headed to the last place I knew you were." Her hands began to tremble. "Where is he?"

CB took her hands in his. "I don't know. Please don't stop being careful."

Flossie took several deep breaths. She continued on with her story. With pride she told about her son and how smart he was with numbers. Then she told her deepest secret. She never spoken to anyone about that damned circumcision and what it meant. Her brother didn't react at all.

"So?"

"So the man is a lying Jewish bastard. He passed himself off as a good Christian man."

"You passed yourself off as a lady. Ain't it just about the same?"

Flossie became Julia in two words. "Absolutely not."

CB sat very still. After a bit, he said, "You are my big sister, and we come from the same place. Just don't forget a high horse can buck. Has this man done anything wrong? Has he beat you? Neglected you? Sounds like he's deservin' some sort of forgiveness."

The siblings sat in silence. Then Flossie was back. "Oh hell, CB, I can't fool you. Just because a chicken has wings doesn't mean it can fly." She smiled. "Mama used to say that. I've spent my whole grown life trying to flap those

108

wings and I'm going to keep on trying. At least it got me into the hen house." She went on to explain the society of the church and how important it was for her. "Oh, if only Mama could see me now. Her work paid off."

It was CB's time to talk. He told her about the checker games and what happened afterwards. Then he told her about the unspendables and Jack's idea. She sat quietly, taking in the thought.

"Do you really think I could sell those things without drawing suspicion?"

"Your church ladies wear jewelry that is mighty fancy. Where do they buy 'em? "

"Some of the women have family pieces. Others say they go up to Houston. There is one good jeweler here on the island, but nobody likes him. Mr. Goldstein sells things far too high, and his mother is just plain nosey. If she sees anyone wearing something from their shop, she'll make a point to tell the world that it was bought from 'my Marty, such a fine boy'. Most of the ladies call him 'Marty Mark-up'. I call him 'Mama's Marty'."

"Does anyone buy from just people?"

"Of course. Sometimes rich women sell their things when they have to hide money problems from their husbands. New clothes and furniture can add up. Sometimes the husbands make their wives sell things to punish them. When that happens, the jewelry goes cheap."

"Are you rich?"

"Oh my Lord, no. That husband of mine is tighter than the bark on a tree. Everyone has seen my old furniture and worn carpets."

"Soooo, you might need to raise some cash for new things?" CB crooked his head sideways and cut half a grin.

"Well, I just might." She matched his tone and his look. They both started laughing. "I can't keep bringing fruit and you can't be seen behind the church. Mrs. Gaithers might want to baptize you on the spot. What can we do?"

"What about Missus Myra?"

"What about her?" Flossie couldn't figure out where this was going.

"Missus Myra is on the docks all the time. She's right as rain. Could you trust her with being part of this?"

"Well," she intoned back, "She did keep her word about you and me. Except for being the talk of the town, what with letting her hellions run wild and all, she has a good name. What's the return? That might get her in, her being poor and all."

"Sounds like you've been living with a counting man too long," he grinned.

"Cash buys carpets. There has to be something to show for me selling the family jewels!"

"Oh, my darlin' sister, you are something else. How does this sound? Find out what Marty Mark-up's percentage is. That'll be the take for you two to split. You talk with Myra and I'll let her know when we will get back. If she's willing, you get the plans working while I am gone."

After another big hug, CB walked to the outer door. "You forget something, sissy?"

"No." and with a giant grin she handed him the rest of the oranges she'd promised. This time the cloth sack held no note. Written words were unneeded. With a quick look both ways, CB skedaddled down the way. She blew out the lantern and no one noticed Julia returning the Sunday School table and chairs. She walked home with shivery arms even though there was no chill in the air whatsoever. Could this be what living felt like? Could she forgive her husband? Could she forgive herself?

***

Supper that evening was going smoothly. Ike was telling his son about the numbers of the day. The boy was exceptionally chatty about his recent round of marbles at school. Julia had a pineapple upside-down cake for desert. It was a delicious ending to a good meal.

"Let me get the coffee," said Julia. Returning from the stove her shoe caught the edge of the dining room carpet and she stumbled. She screamed as a full pot of brew went all over the place. Everyone ran for rags to sponge up the mess. The table was moved, the carpet rolled, and dragged outside. Once opened, they all noticed the coffee stain was spread wide. Julia worked hard to clean the rug, and it was left to dry overnight. By morning the brown stain was set in the wool tufts. Ike put the carpet back in place under the table.

"We will need to get a new one," was all she said.

Chapter 18

GOIN' FISHIN'

The Shoe was beneath Julia. She knew she needed to talk with Myra, but, she wasn't about to walk in that neighborhood. She heard about Mexicans living there, or at least somebody saw one once.

"My Ikey beat Junior at Picking Plums." Few Guild heads raised. Bragging about children around the sorting table was standard conversation. "He wants to go over there to play. Ada, where does Missus Myra live?"

That ploy got The Shoe's address on a slip of paper tucked into her pocket. The next day she stopped by the post office, sending Myra a note. *"Please come visit me at the church. Julia."* She didn't have to wait long. Myra visited the Guild room within the week. Julia saw her in the doorway.

"Why, Myra," said Julia, "So good to see you. Has my Ikey been too much of a bother for you? Do you need me to come fetch him?"

Myra stared at her. What in Glory's sake was she talking about? Julia set down her work, nodded to the ladies, and swooped Myra into the hall. She jerked her head back at the hen house. "I told them that Young Ike wanted to play marbles at your house. That's how I got your address."

"All you had to do was ask Aunt Ada to find me."

Julia was aghast at that idea. Ada, bless her heart, loved to talk. What she needed to tell Myra could not go anywhere. The women headed out onto the street and turned the corner. Mid-block Julia stopped.

"I know your situation. Everybody knows your situation. You're poor."

Myra's eyes widened. This certainly was not news to her.

"I have a way to help you", Julia continued.

"Excuse me, Miss Flossie Mae Ledbetter. I do not need your charity, you little stuck up hypocrite." Myra swung around, barely missing Julia with her reticule, and strode off, head high.

"Myra, please, I'm sorry." It was Julia's tone that stopped her. It was the first time since they shared news of Cletus' arrival that a truly real voice came out of her mouth. Myra turned, hands on hips.

"What." It was a statement, not a question.

"My brother has a business proposition for the both of us."

"And..." Myra's tone showed interest.

"I could use the money, too. Ike won't let me buy anything new. I have remade my wedding dress so many times, you'd think we were poor. Oh, sorry, no offense."

"None taken." Myra started to smile. Julia couldn't help being the way she was. "So what's the deal? Whatever in this world could we do for Sure Foot?"

Julia smiled. "Everything."

***

The *Sallie Lou* returned within the month. Myra called 'sweet cakes'" on her rounds. Sure Foot bought her treats, passing the jewelry with the coins for payment, and the pockets on her apron got heavy. For five days the women met in the narthex. After a brief chat, they would hold hands in prayer. After "Amen", Myra would head to The Shoe to bake. Julia piously slid her hands into her pockets and headed back to the Guild room. "Missus Myra is learning to pray."

"Hmmm," was all that came from Ada. She knew Myra and wondered what she was really learning. Maybe child behaving. That was a lesson she could use. Whatever lesson it was, it all ended as soon as it began.

Marty Mark-up loved the pearl stick pin and two brooches when Julia visited his jewelry shop. Other ladies of the community sold to him before, and he knew he could offer low. Julia was counting on it.

"You have the finest quality here. What price are you asking?"

She gave him an outlandishly high number. "What will you offer?"

When he countered with a lower amount, Julia feigned insult and left with a sniff. Now she knew his margin and added that percentage to the asking price.

***

"Ladies, I have to confess a problem." Everybody looked up. Julia wouldn't confess to eating dinner, let alone tell her business. She had the room's attention.

Hook.

"Last month I spilled a full pot of coffee on my dining room carpeting and ruined it." The women murmured tones of sympathy. "The stain is horrible. I have tried everything, and won't come out." The murmuring became understanding. They all had wool dining carpets and staining was a big worry.

"I need to replace it, but I feel so guilty. My beloved husband works hard for us. I don't want to take house budget for this. Does anyone have a suggestion on how to get some cash?" Her eyes dropped to her lap. "You know, quietly? My Ike would be so embarrassed if he knew I was trying to raise money." Her eyes were glistening when she raised her head.

"Can you sell anything? I sold my mother-in-law's silver." Hmm, so that's how Constable Turner's wife got that new parlor set.

Line.

"I, um, have some jewelry." Julia looked hopeful. "Does anyone know if you can sell that?"

"Is it quality?" Mrs. Gaither spoke up.

"My mother's." Looking down, she fiddled with her dress. Julia never spoke about her family. Ears perked. A single tear rolled down her cheek. "She died when I was very young. I have her things."

"Oh. You poor dear. We didn't know. "

Julia took out her handkerchief and dabbed her eyes. "My dear daddy, God rest his soul, gave them to me as a wedding gift from her. He said it was the best way she could send her love from heaven." She gulped. "I know my mama would want me to take care of my problem. She was always so house-proud. There are, um, some diamonds and other pretty things."

Sinker.

Mrs. Gaithers became an easy fish. Julia sold her the diamond brooch, and hinted she would be willing to sell more of 'poor Mother's things'. Other Guild members swam around the bait, and several bit. The pieces were beautiful, they all had to admit.

Set.

Some of the unsellables were sold. All Julia had to do now was divvy up the money. The Island City Savings Bank exchanged bills into coins, handing them to her in a muslin drawstring bag.

"Ma'am, are you sure you will be all right with this? I suggest you hold the money close to you. We don't want a robbery on our hands." The bank man pushed the sack across the marble surface of the teller's cage. Julia was shocked at the weight and took his advice. Even so, she was afraid the jingling could be heard as she walked straight home. No one was there, thank heavens. She carefully counted out the money in their proper rows. She knew gold coins would draw attention, so she requested silver only. It never occurred to her that silver dollars were about four times larger than gold pieces until it was too late. Ah well, next time…She hoped there was a next time. This was so thrilling. She wrapped each stack with butcher paper and tied them snug with string. She hid her take in the back corner of her corset drawer and CB's and Myra's in the garden shed. She knew Ike would never go there. He always thought gardening was women's work. She ordered her dining carpeting the next day.

Another post to The Shoe set the time and location for the next meeting. This time Myra needed to come to the Jameson's house, and would she please bring her basket. Myra wrinkled her brow at that one. Sure Foot handed her the jewels with his sweets money and she made sure Julia got everything with the praying. What did she need her basket for?

Julia greeted her with genuine enthusiasm. Once the obligatory pound cake and coffee were served, Julia reached behind the settee and brought out the two wrapped bundles she'd fetched from the shed. Myra smiled.

"I see you have sweets for my basket." The women started laughing. Neither could believe they'd done it.

"Yes ma'am." Julia handed her the parcels. Myra dropped both of them on her lap with a plop.

"My Heavens, what have you given me?"

"Coins. I figured they would be easier to spend. Forgot about the bulk."

"I guess you did." She picked up the smaller of the two packages. "Mine? Guess I'll be paying my bills with silver dollars for a while."

"Yes, I guess you will. I have the same. It was more than enough to replace my carpet." She gestured to the dining room and its new finery. "Ike never even noticed the newness. I told him I cleaned it good. The other bundle is for CB. Is he in port yet?"

"Soon." She hefted the larger one, weighing it in her hand. She wondered how many traveling men this represented. She smiled. She never handled so much money in her life. Carefully she put the cash in her basket. It was heavy.

"Myra, would you do this again if we are asked?" Julia tried to speak calmly, but didn't succeed.

"You might have to spill another pot of coffee…maybe on your settee." Myra grinned and picked up her basket. "You rightly can't replace another rug."

"What are you going to buy?" Julia smiled at her.

"I am never going to wash clothes again. I already started taking everything to Wha Fung's Chinese Laundry on account. You can't imagine what my wash day was like."

When Julia showed her the door, she stepped shyly in front of Myra. "We have had so much fun. You know my story. I trust you so much. May I call you sister?"

"Well now, I think I like that, but Sure Foot can't be my brother. He's sweet on me."

"You?"

"Could be." Myra blushed. "I have no idea what he's thinking, though. No man would want my passel of brats, even if he is a sailor."

"Well, between you, me and the gatepost, I think you two seem like you belong together. You're the same size and he's not so homely when you get to know him. CB has a heart of gold…and jewels." Both women laughed at the joke.

"By the way," said Myra. "Next time you come to my house."

"The Mexicans?" Julia made a face. "Is it safe?"

"What in God's name are you talking about? What Mexicans?"

"Someone at Guild said they saw Mexicans in your neighborhood. You know you can't trust them."

Myra laughed. She was so glad she never earned a roost in the hen house.

"Do you think my Uncle Harry would let me live on a bad street? He'd move us quicker than a whip stitch if he thought we were in danger. As for Mexicans, the family three houses down does have a light skinned colored man for their yard work. Mister John workin' in his gardening hat must be what one of the ladies saw. You know, sometimes gossip is what it is and nothing more." Myra set down her basket. Putting a hand on each of Julia's shoulders, she spoke. "We are sisters. Come to my house." With a quick kiss on the cheek, Myra and her basket were gone. Julia never had a sister. She liked the idea.

Chapter 19

REDEMPTION

Cletus B. Ledbetter was working himself up one bad reputation in the taverns. His bragging mouth and loud ramblin's about days gone by made him an unwelcome guest after the bottle'd been passed twice. He got mean, with a rough way of settling his many scores. A man could 'bout look at him cross-eyed and he'd reach for his belt. He could snap it like a bull whip. It was almost like he took pride in his meanness. He sure did take pride in that belt and his ways with it. When he was just starting an evening of drinking, he would make bets with the men on his ability to flick the strap, wrap it around his glass, and pull his whiskey toward him. The regulars knew his tricks, but there was always a stranger to be had. The bet would be made. If he could move his glass without spilling it, the mark would have to buy him a bottle. If he did spill it, he would buy the man his next round. Cletus never once bought another drink for the rest of the night, but as he would get drunk and ugly, the belt would come off to fight. He loved to whup up a stranger. When the regulars saw him reach for his buckle the second time, they would get clear. The men would try to pull the stranger out, but more than once, the lash would cut skin.

Julia always kept a wary eye out as she went about town. The wharves had many whiskey joints around them, so she rarely visited her husband's office. Julia knew CB was out to sea, and felt sure Myra would notify her the next time the *Sallie Lou* was in port. At home Ike never mentioned he missed her visits. He did talk about the counting house with Young Ike, telling him how important schooling was if he was going to work in the office someday. Their son was bright with numbers. Ike would take him into the side parlor after dinner to review daily accountings, giving his son additions to cypher. Julia was glad Ike had Young Ike to talk to, as she showed no interest in his day's work. She was very thankful her husband did not keep whiskey in their house. The memory of what-was had long been put aside for the keeping of the what-is. Now, with Daddy in town, the what-was seeped into her daily thoughts.

Mama never knew she and CB could hear the lashin' and the screamin'. Julia knew what the belt felt like, but she never knew what happened next. Daddy would drag Mama into the back room, her crying and all. Then they heard nothing. Much later Mama would come out on the porch, herself all a mess, and call them in for supper. Daddy never came to the table.

"Your father's taking a nap," was her standard response. It wasn't until Julia was grown that she realized what he had done.

When the *Sallie* was in port the boys would frequent the *Fat Maude*, *Bastard Bill*, and, Sure Foot's favorite, *The Title House*. When asked why, Sure Foot would tell the story about coming there at age nine when he was sayin' good bye to his daddy, and his daddy thought the sign read Tittie House.

"Let's go to the Tittie House," he said to the boy. "When you get older, you're gonna like titties, unless you end up some kind of nancy pants." Cletus looked at CB. "Son, you ain't gonna be no nancy pants, are you?" CB pulled him through the swinging doors. He didn't know what a nancy pants was, but he did know what titties were, and he was willing to like them.

"It's all right, Daddy, I like titties." At this part of the story, the listeners would start to chuckle. "I like the titties on fat girls. You know, Daddy, the jiggly kind." The thought of a little boy talkin' like that with his pa would get the men to laughing. "Here's to nipples," Sure Foot would call out with his mug held high, "For without them, titties would be pointless." The men at the Title House would all down their whiskey and call for more. The barman knew the night would be profitable every time the bowlegged sailor and his colored friend came into town.

It had been two full routings since the boys had to lay low. They both felt time was passed enough, and they were back into the movin' business, full swing. Thanks to Flossie, they had a way of taking care of the unspendables. Today Jack carried the checkerboard into the *Fat Maude*. Sure Foot would be along as soon as he got the Captain settled in with his tray and brandy.

"Hoy, Jack, you got your mouthpiece with you?" Clarisse, the barmaid, first cousin to Maude, never was one to care about color. When the ships came to port, even the Chinese got served if they would sit in the back. Couldn't have them sittin' by the windows, you know. Jack and his white friend would play checkers and spin stories. Jack would blow the harmonica to start the evening. The white boy would sing some bawdy songs. Eventually, Jack would stop playing and start singing. His tenor voice could sound like the notes of the mouth organ. At the end of the song, the tavern would go wild with stompin' and whistlin'. They always finished the singing with 'The Golden Gate'. The words told of a place where "pleasures never die: And angel bands our coming wait, to greet us at the golden gate." For those in the know, this was the signal to start watching the checkers to see if you would get to go to the gold.

"Yes, Miss Clarisse, I do. Have you seen Sure Foot anywhere? He's got the checkers. Can't rightly play without my man and the men."

Clarisse laughed. "You're a smart one. Can't get kinged without an army of men."

Jack thought it was fine that a white woman would joke with him. He smiled at her. She was plump in a soft sort of way. However, he'd never seen hair lookin' like that. Today she had an unnatural yellow stripe down the side.

"Miss Clarisse, excuse me for noticing, but what happened to your hair? Did you get into the paint?"

"Shoot, boy. I got hennaed yesterday. What ya think? Ya like it?" She grinned and patted her curls. "I know it ain't as colorful as the oyster gal's red hair, but yella's good enough for me." Jack felt a blush rise at the mention of the red-headed fish gal. He knew better than to say anything else. It wasn't right for a colored man to answer a personal question, even if she did ask. She kinda reminded him of an older sister, the way she was always good to him.

"You want something to drink? On the house, of course."

"Just beer. I'll set up my board over there in the corner, if you don't mind. Let me wet my whistle, and I'll play you a thank you tune."

Several mugs and many songs later, the place was full and Sure Foot still wasn't there. This was the day for their night work. Jack couldn't show it, but he was getting nervous. Where was his partner? All of a sudden the place went dead still.

"There's that goddam nigger again. What is he doin' blowin' on that thing?"

Clarisse was big enough to pull a beer, but definitely not big enough to fight a man. She knew trouble when she heard it, and knew the best thing she could do would be to git, and she did.

"Last time I saw you, I told you I didn't want to see your black ass again." Cletus walked slowly across the room as the men cleared out. They knew what might come next, and felt they could do their drinking elsewhere.

"You steal that mouth organ, nigger? You gotta be too poor to buy one."

Jack now realized he was a trapped rat, sitting in the

corner. There was no one else in the room. Cletus already figured out he was gonna have some fun tonight and knew he could sell the harmonica for a good time of drinkin' and whorin'.

"No, sir, I didn't steal it. My captain gave it to me."

"Boy, don't you talk all la-de-da to me."

Jack had forgotten to speak common. He changed over to, "I's be goin, suh. Sorry to 'sturb you."

Cletus leaned over and grabbed both of Jack's wrists with one hand. With the other he tore the harmonica away. Jack felt something boil in him that could only be the anger of his ancestors. Cletus jerked Jack sideways, knocking him off his stool, twisting him down to his knees. He'd done this before, knowing he couldn't win a fight with a standing opponent, especially a tall one. He then gave the young man a full force kick in his stomach. Jack lay stunned, his air gone.

"Get up, nigger. I'll teach you fancy talk." Cletus calmly pocketed his prize and went for his belt buckle. Jack gasped and tried to do as he was told. *Oh, God, where was Sure Foot?* Cletus kicked him again, this time in his side. Jack fell forward and lay there, unable to breathe. Cletus pulled off his belt. He knew whippin' a nigger would make the whoring even better. Oh, how he missed his wife, but this would have to do. He snapped the belt in the air above Jack's back.

"You are one lazy, stealin' nigger. Looks like you need more than talkin' lessons. You need manners lessons." The belt met flesh. Jack screamed. He tried to move.

"Shut up, nigger, or I'll shut you up." Cletus kicked him in the ribs and bones cracked. He flicked the belt so it tore the shirt and skin. Cletus liked what he was doing. It made him want. Another lash, another tear. *That goddam nigger's got no right bein' in a white woman's place.* Lash. *Goddam nigger's got no right havin' that mouth organ.* Lash. *Goddam nigger's got no right tryin' to talk white.*

Lash.

After a while Cletus got bored and walked to the bar to steal a bottle. Without looking back, he put on his belt and left, searching for a woman who would appreciate how worked up he was. Damn, he was one fine man. He'd show her a thing or two.

Jack crawled out of the bar, his shredded shirt soaked with sweat and blood. He made it to the alley wishin' he could pass out. He lay on his good side, curled up like a dying dog, waiting. It was Clarisse who found him. She crumpled to the ground, crying, and took Jack's head into her lap, rocking him. That's when Jack began to cry, too. He cried for his pain, he cried for his mama, and he cried for his harmonica. Jack knew he would heal, but he also knew he could never have another gift like the one his captain gave him. This man had called him 'son' and now, he knew the Captain would never trust him with gifts of value again.

"Oh, my God, I am so sorry. I am so sorry." Clarisse crooned and rocked him. "I ran to get Maude. He was upstairs, eating supper. He came down after he et, but it was too late. The man was gone." Jack did not realize until later exactly what Clarisse said.

"I sent him out to find your bowlegged friend. Let's hope he does real soon. Will you let me look at your back?"

Jack sniffed, nodded, and tried to sit up. "Oh, God, my ribs," he moaned. His back hurt worse than fire burn. Clarisse helped him. She then saw what she hadn't seen before. The belt had shredded his shirt and the threads were born into the broken skin. The blood made it look like red ribbons were growing out of his brown back. She was only able to step away a few paces before she vomited. She quickly wiped the mess off her mouth with the back of her hand so Jack wouldn't see. There was a rain barrel down the way a bit. After splashing her face and hands, she took off her apron and got it soaking. Clarisse put the whole dripping mess on his back. Jack howled.

It was the scream that brought Maude and Sure Foot running.

"Jesus Christ, man." Maude watched as the blood seeped through the wet apron, making a hideous tracing on the cloth. He lifted the fabric. Jack gritted his teeth, hissing in pain. This time it was Sure Foot who, reaching for his friend, held his head. Both boys sobbed.

"Daddy?"

"Yes."

After a bit, the men got the young man to his feet and into the back kitchen of the tavern. Sure Foot and Maude took a table in front, just in case some drinkers were there. Clarisse laid Jack out belly down on the butcher table and very carefully fed him her best whiskey. Since Jack wasn't used to anything best, let alone whiskey, he was soon lulled. She then cut his shirt up the side seams so that she could remove those hideous ribbons. She murmured the twenty-third psalm as she worked. When she was done, she started in on the Lord's Prayer and then went into cussin' the 'goddam son-of-a-bitch who did this'. As she pulled the threads out of the wounds, she suddenly realized she'd kissed the back of his head like she would a baby child. Hmmm, thank goodness no one saw that. She dribbled some more whiskey into the side of Jack's mouth so he wouldn't know it either. He didn't need to have the thought of a white woman's lips on him. Then she went back to thread pickin'.

***

Maude poured each of them a finger of his mid-line whiskey. Maude spoke first.

"Is Cletus your daddy?"

"Yes, but he doesn't know I'm here. He ran across Jack at the *Bastard* a while back when we were playing. He got real ugly real quick and the barkeep distracted him enough so we could high tail it. He was so fired up about

Jack that he didn't notice me when we ran."

"Cletus has been nothin' but trouble since he showed up in this town. Do you know about his belt?"

Sure Foot looked into his glass. "Yes sir, I do."

"He do that to you?"

"Has."

"Oh, Jesus."

"Mama, too."

Maude stared hard at Sure Foot.

"You want him dead?"

"Yes." He didn't say it was because of his sister. No one could know about that. "Jack is like my brother. Would you really kill that ass-wipe?"

"Clarisse saw what happened. You go talk to her. I'll stay here and mind the bar."

Sure Foot walked into the kitchen just as Clarisse was putting a poultice on the cuts.

"Tell me, girl. Did Jack cause this?"

"Oh, Jesus, no! He was making his music, waitin' for you, and that devil man walked in and started at him right away. Didn't think a colored man should have such a nice mouth piece. I was hiding in the stairwell and heard Jack tell him his captain gave it to him. Didn't mean nothin' to Cletus. He pinned him with one hand and jerked out the harmonica with the other. I ran to get Maude when I heard the boy scream."

"He kept the harmonica?"

"Yes, I'm pretty sure he did."

"You have any idea where he went?"

"He goes down to Post Office Street and sees Missus Elizabeth when he can."

"That old whore? They say she's dirty."

"It's his money," grunted Clarisse. "You think he'll sell the mouth piece for a better woman?"

"Maybe... and more whiskey. Clarisse, you tend Jack good. Maude and I got business to do."

"You know I will. I am so sorry I couldn't stop the son-of-a-bitch. You tell Maude I'll get out front as soon as I am done here."

Sure Foot told Maude everything. Maude ran a clean house and was used to telling his patrons where the girls were since there were none under his roof. He knew just where to find Missus Elizabeth and the men were soon out on the street. As they walked they asked whoever they met if anyone had bought a harmonica in the last hour. No one had. Several corner turns later they were at the house of Missus Catherine. Everyone call it The Cat House, for obvious reasons. Sure Foot waited while Maude went in to talk to Catherine. He was soon back with news. Cletus was upstairs with Elizabeth, passed out drunk from the bottle he stole. Missus Elizabeth would be much obliged if Maude would remove him. The man was too drunk to enjoy her company and she wasn't strong enough to haul him off her bed. A girl has to support herself, you know. They both went back into the House.

"Heaven's sake, boy, you look like that pile of dog shit upstairs. He your pa?" Missus Catherine gave Sure Foot the eye.

"Leave him alone, he can't help who sired him." Maude knew the Cat House was a nasty box of gossip and didn't want Sure Foot's name dragged through manure. He and his colored side-kick brought business to the *Fat* and he didn't want any mess spread to his place. The two climbed the steps.

Elizabeth was sitting in the side chair, dressed in an old pink silk wrapper. Her hair was loose and streaks of gray were trying to win over the brown that was left. She nodded toward the bed.

"Can you take out the trash? Can't do business this way."

Sure Foot went straight for the belt. That damned thing would burn in hell before it ever hurt another man.

Once the belt was off Cletus and strapped around his own middle, Sure Foot started on the pockets. He dug, patted, felt. The harmonica was not there. He turned to Maude, tilting his head toward the whore.

"You know what I want. It's gone. Would you be so kind as to inquire?" Maude was in front of the woman in two steps. He tore open her robe. Her old heavy breasts hung low.

"Hold it, you. Ya gotta pay to look."

As quick as a lick Maude grabbed her by the nipples and lifted both sag bags. The harmonica fell from under the left one, down her lap, and onto the floor. Sure Foot snatched it up and put it in his pocket.

"I was just keeping it safe." The old whore cocked her head at Maude and smiled. Her front teeth were missing. "You can understand, him with no money. You wanna stay awhile?"

Resisting the urge to slap her stupid face, he dropped her tits instead. He turned to Sure Foot.

"Let's clean up this room."

The men each took one of Cletus' arms and got him on his feet. The bed was soaked with the rest of the stolen whiskey and what smelled like pee. As they dragged him across the room and out the door, Elizabeth tied the ragged silk around her and headed straight to the task of stripping and turning the mattress, muttering every curse she could remember. *No goddam piss ant was gonna stop her from a night of work. She may be old, but she had men who would pay something for her company.* She sprinkled cologne on the ticking and smoothed on yesterday's sheets.

Cletus was too drunk to walk, so the men dragged him backwards down the steps. His boots banged every steps and Catherine was squallin' as they got to the bottom. Ignoring her noise, they just kept hauling 'til they got out the door and down off the front stoop. Then they dropped their load. Yep, he was the one who peed.

128

Sure Foot turned to Maude. "I am sorry to get you into this."

"Hell, don't be. I'm just getting' a rat out of my saloon. That crazy-ass man ruined many a profitable night for me." He looked straight at Sure Foot. "You still want him gone?"

"Yes." He would do anything to keep Flossie safe.

Maude scratched his left ear. Damn, did he pick up a louse in that whore's room? "I can kill him but we can't leave him lay. People already know we dragged him out of the Cat House."

Sure Foot stood quiet, lookin' down at the man he once called Daddy. He knew he had to tell Maude about the checker game.

"Maude, do you know why Jack and I play checkers?"

"To pass time between songs?"

"No. We're doing business. When I tell you this, I will understand if you kick us out of the *Fat* for good."

"You runnin' flim-flam?"

"No sir, we're runnin' men." Sucking air, Sure Foot told Maude about the game, the barrels and the stow-away men they hid. He knew he had to do this because of what was coming next.

"What you think about getting him," he couldn't say 'Daddy', "into one of those barrels. Seal the bung and let him stay asleep. A few days out, he can go over with the rest of the garbage. I'll pull the stop to make sure it sinks. That's what we do with all the trash."

Maude found the louse and squinched it between his fingers. He flicked the leavin's on Cletus's stained crotch. "Damn it, that's some kind of go-to. You two pulled my leg real good. I thought those men liked my liquor and your singin'. Didn't know they wanted more. Hell, you brought me payin' customers, I'm square." He grinned at Sure Foot. "Let's go for a little walk. Good with you?"

So the two men went along with their very drunk companion. They walked and dragged him in and out, around about the streets, slowly working their way to the docks. When they got to the *Sallie Lou's* berth, Sure Foot left the bar owner with his charge. Maude leaning against a crate with Cletus flopped down like they were too far gone to move. That was a common sight late of an evening.

An odd rumble across the way alerted Maude. There was a keg 'bout four some feet high rolling toward him. Behind it was Sure Foot pushing it with all his might. All you could see was his head and shoulders. Maude hadn't realized the young man's size. He just might have to call him Short Foot next time. He went over to give a hand.

"Don't. Men might notice you doin' my work and talk." Sure Foot finished the rolling up to the crate. There he stopped and pried off the end piece with a claw hammer he had picked up along the way. Maude looked down at Cletus. He pulled out his silver pocket flask.

"Hold his head. We're gonna give this man a good-night toddy."

Sure Foot took the flask. "You hold him. I hate him too much to touch him."

Maude squatted down, and held open the drunk's mouth. Leaning over, Sure Foot splashed onto his father's face and lips all the man ever wanted or loved. The liquor that fueled his whippin's, his hatin's, and his woman hurtin' was now going up his nose and down his throat. Cletus gagged and swallowed. Sure Foot drained the flask and stood up straight. Without a word, Maude pulled the belt from around CB's waist. He tied the hands of Cletus B. Ledbetter with his own strap and tumbled him into the open end of the keg. Both men ignored the thunk and groan that came from within. Sure Foot lifted on the end piece and Maude secured it with the hammer. Then he gave the bung a strike, practically buried it.

"Son, we better roll this up the plank. I'll give you a

hand. If your men say something, you tell them that Jack is with Clarisse." Maude was tellin' the truth.

If anyone saw them getting the barrel on board, no one said a word. They put it with the others in the hold. It was then that Maude noticed the P/K markings. None of the other kegs were marked that way. Damn, Sure Foot was one smart fella. They left the ship and went back to the *Fat*. Cletus ran out of air before first mess.

Clarisse strapped up Jack's back and ribs with ointment and linens. He was still on the butcher table, only now he was on his side with a pillow and a quilt. He was snoring the snore of contentment. Clarisse had taken chairs and put the backs all around the table, just in case he rolled, and he looked like someone's tucked-in child. She was out front, shooing away the straggling dreamers who were still waiting for that promised checker game. Sure Foot went straight to the back, and when he saw his friend was good, joined Maude. Without a word, it was agreed they would never speak of this night again. When Clarisse asked, Maude said they'd gotten the old drunk out of town and he would not be coming back. She pulled a round of beer. The three sat together in the empty tavern and quietly drank to the day.

Jack started screaming. The dream of the lash was too real. Sure Foot tore the crib of chairs away from his friend and shook him until he had wide eyes.

"Man, you've been through hell. Don't jolt yourself. Miss Clarisse here has tended you best she can. Do you think you can sit?"

Jack stared at Sure Foot. Things started coming back.

"Oh God, what will I do? My harmonica is gone. Cap'n will never trust me again."

"Come on, man, try to sit." Sure Foot gently helped him, swinging his legs over the side of the table. After Jack was up, Sure Foot planted himself directly in front of him and reached in his pocket. Pulling out the harmonica, he said, "Maude got it back."

Jack stared. "How?" was all he said. He put it in his pants pocket.

Maude spoke. "You needn't ever worry about that piece of shit again. He won't be coming back to town."

Clarisse knew the best thing for the situation was to boil some coffee. As quick as she could get the eggshell in, the cups were poured. Jack drank, sitting quietly, looking from face to face. He knew, right then, he was safe. He also knew the woman had kissed him as she mended him. That he kept in his heart. After Clarisse served up some pot roast with gravy bread, he felt he could move. Maude brought down his oldest shirt for Jack. The two sailors thanked their good friends and headed to the ship. As they walked, Sure Foot told Jack everything.

***

Sure Foot had news for Flossie. The next morning he spoke to Myra. "Tell her she is safe. Tell her Cletus B. Ledbetter will never come back here. He is dead. He died tied up with his own belt. That's fittin', don't you think?"

He kept his head down and did not say another word.

Three days later, somewhere on the way south to Havana, Jack pulled the bung of that foul cask and they rolled it overboard, watching it sink. The other sailors wondered why the lads were singing 'Joy To the World' and it wasn't even that close to Christmas.

Chapter 20

OLD TIME RELIGIONS

Julia had a horrible headache. She was dozing half reclined on her settee with a shawl on backwards, thrown over her like a shroud. The ghosts were everywhere. Daddy, Flossie, CB, Mama. Julia Marie Smythe Jameson did not exist. She was a ghost, too. "Oh, Mama. Why? Why? Why? Why is it so hard?" Her spoken words startled her, making her head throb. Sitting up, she rearranged her covering to its appropriate place, around her shoulders. No one was going to see her in her own house, but it didn't matter. Propriety was propriety. "Oh, Mama, I am so tired. Why am I here?"

Ever since her alliance with Myra, Julia doubted everything about herself. Myra Gallaway's life was hard, but she always had a smile for everyone. Those five children were her strength, her purpose. Julia's mama trained her to be a lady, to pass, but taught her nothing more. Flossie Ledbetter was dead, killed off with desperation and hope. Julia Marie Smythe Jameson was deader, a woman without purpose covered with the ashes of fakery.

Myra promised to keep her secret. CB told her to get off her high horse. Ike never knew. After the visitor from New York stepped on her front porch all those many years ago, Julia never, ever spoke of her own history. She left their marriage bed that night, breaking her vows because some strange woman came to her door.

"Oh dear God, what have I done?" Julia stood up. The movement made the headache flash behind her eyes. Drawing the shawl tighter, she walked to the middle of the parlor and looked at all she'd worked so very hard for. The rooms, the house, the church and all it represented...*Oh Mama, I'm so lonely on this high horse, this statue I built for myself.* Myra and CB were more family than her own husband, the man she hated for being just like her...*just like her.*

Julia walked into the bedroom she'd abandoned before their son was born. The family Bible was on the nightstand by the side of the bed where she would have slept. Ike carried it to church every Sunday, returning it to the empty table. She sat down and picked up the book. The envelope was still there. Shaking, she opened it and read aloud part of its contents.

"Will you have this man to be your husband, to live together in holy matrimony? Will you love him, comfort him, honor and keep him in sickness and in health, and forsaking all others, be faithful to him as long as you both shall live?" Returning the paper, she reached for the single pillow on the double bed. Holding it to her like a long absent lover, she sobbed until exhaustion. *Mama, Mama, what have I done?*

Ike found her sound asleep on his bed, the pillow still in her arms. Whatever happened could wait. He very gently covered her with the day spread from the quilt rack at the foot of the bed. He shut the bedroom door and walked out.

The two Ikes supped on hobo food, thick slices of bread and cold beans from a can. Young Ike mentioned, "Mother wouldn't like this, would she?" as he licked his spoon, grin on his face.

"Your mother likes her kind of food, us hoboes like ours." Ike spooned more beans onto another piece of bread, folded it in half and savored his sandwich. Son imitated father. There was a cough by the hallway.

"Can you open another tin?" Julia was standing there, her hair all straggling down, face flushed with sleep and crying. "I know how to eat beans and bread, too."

The shocked Ikes served their hobo queen.

"This tastes so good," she said. "I used to like bean

sandwiches. May I have some more?"

Her husband watched as she ate three plates full. After Julia scraped up the last bits with her bread crust, Ike turned to their son. "Hoboes don't need to work numbers tonight. It's time for you to wash your face and get ready for bed."

Young Ike didn't know what was happening, but knew better than to disobey his father's instructions. He was soon in his bed, his lamp extinguished. There he lay, listening with the intense curiosity of every child put to bed early. The soft sounds from the parlor eventually lulled him to sleep. Whatever they were talking about was between them alone.

"My name if Flossie Mae Ledbetter. I come from dirt floor trash. My mother is dead, my brother went to sea, and my father hurt me more than anyone has a right to. This was a very long time ago." Julia was whispering on the settee, holding Ike's hand. "I hated you for being a Jew, but you should hate me as well. I am nothing but a fraud, a horrible, mean spirited fraud." The tears started as soon as she sat down. She took out her hanky and patted her cheeks.

"Please forgive me," she continued. "Please forgive me. I am not worthy to be your wife, but I need to know you forgive me before I go."

"Go? Where? Why?" Ike sat there, staring at her.

"I have not honored you, I have not comforted you. I have not been a wife to you."

"That's true. You left me alone."

"I know. I'm sorry."

Ike stood up and started pacing in front of her. "Why, for God's sake, did you do that?" he whispered. "Did I hurt you in any way?"

Ike knelt, cupping her face, Julia softly weeping, keeping her face in her hands. "Damn it, Julia, tell me what I did. Tell me why." His low voice was harsh. He closed his hands around hers and pulled them from her face. The sight of her streaming tears brought on his own. "Look at me, Julia, look at me" he choked. "Tell me what possessed you to abandon me? What in hell did I do?"

"You were born a Jew."

Ike pulled away from her. "Jesus Christ, I can't help that. Have I lived as a Jew? Have I ever been to a temple in this town?" Ike started pacing again. "Have I embarrassed you in front of your precious Methodist ladies?" He spat the denomination. He stopped dead still, staring at her. "Oh my God, you love those women more than you ever loved me. I house you. I clothe you. I feed you, yet you give more attention to any one of those old biddies than you ever thought to give me." Ike was seething. "All because I was born Jew? Well damn you, Julia Flossie, whoever the hell you are. You knew my story from the beginning. I never lied. Now look where we are." Ike walked out of the room, on to the porch. He did not let the screen door slam even though he wanted to rip it from the hinges and break it in half. Taking his handkerchief, he wiped his eyes and blew his nose.

Julia stepped out beside him and took the 'kerchief, ignoring its recent use. "Will you let me talk to you? Will you let me explain?" *Will you forgive?* She gulped, wiped and blew. "Please?"

He took her by the arm and roughly guided her back into the parlor, pulling her down on the settee beside him. "Speak."

Julia told him about everything in her past; the burns, the Mama beatings and the 'naps' afterwards that she knew was so much more. She told how her mama got her the lady lessons, how they were her passage away from her daddy. She explained how she lied her way into society. "My mama gave me everything she could to save me. What she did not teach me was how to love. I think Daddy killed that early on." Julia's voice was becoming calm.

"My dear wife, if only you had told me. I would have understood, I think. I have not liked you, but, do you know? I never stopped loving you." She nodded. "Do you have any living kin at all?"

Julia broke into a tentative smile. "Mama and Daddy are dead, but I do have a brother. You saw him one day."

"When?"

"Remember telling me about the bowlegged man on the wharf? My daddy and my brother were both bowlegged. I had to know who this man was."

Ike was beginning to understand. "So that's why you and the ladies took oranges out on the docks."

"Yes. I needed to find out if he was my baby brother. Oh, Ike, he figured out who I was even though we hadn't seen each other in forever. I couldn't believe it." Her smile spread to her eyes. "We've visited several times."

"How did you do that? You haven't been out on the docks in a long time."

"Missus Myra helped us. We met in the church..."

"The church? How did you pull that one off?" Ike was astonished. "Your church ladies would've had a hay day with that."

Julia looked at her husband. "Would you like a cup of coffee? I could make new."

"I have cakes from the office."

"I know."

***

Several cups and many tears later Julia shared almost everything. Ike took her hands.

"Do you want to be my wife?"

"Yes."

"You and I are of common spirit."

"Yes."

Ike leaned in and kissed her tear-streaked cheeks, first the left and then the right. Sitting back he wiped her face with firm strokes. She snuffled and took the handkerchief from him, wiping her nose.

"Will you let me stay?" Julia looked him directly in the eyes. "I know it will be hard, but could we start fresh? I am so tired of the lies."

"Missus Flossie Mae Ledbetter Julia Marie Smythe, you are my wife and always will be." Ike was holding her hands again.

She gave them a shake and a squeeze. "Please call me Julia Jameson."

"Missus Julia Jameson, you are my wife and always will be." They both started laughing.

"Mister Isaac Jacoby, will you be my husband?"

"Please call me Ike. Yes, I will be your husband. I am Old Testament, you are New. We are the Good Book."

Julia stood up and tiptoed into the nursery, retrieving the pillow from her bed. Ike took her hand and led her into their bedroom. Julia found the small enameled box right where she left it many years ago. She excused herself to the privy closet where she uncorked the tiny vinegar bottle, soaked the sponge, and put the safety in its place. This time she let him touch her back as much as he wanted. There are some secrets not worth keeping, and some that are.

So she did.

Chapter 21

PECKER NECKS

All the kids wanted one, at least all the boys did. The girls just giggled. Pecker necks, pecker neck chickens, also called turkens, but Young Ike liked the shock value of 'pecker neck'. James Williams was giving away the chicks after school. He said they could start a club and all you needed to do was feed them table scraps, easy as pie, if there was any left. He said they were good scratchers and liked bugs and worms, too. Easy keeping, no problem. Ike came home with three, two hens and a rooster, and set the crate on the kitchen table.

"You have what in that?" His mother just stared at him, pointing.

"Pecker necks."

"I beg your pardon, young man. I will wash your mouth out with soap with that kind of language." Julia was already heading to the sideboard to get her dishrag.

"No, Mother, I'm not talking nasty, I'm talking fowl." Young Ike's started snickering at his own joke. "We are the proud owners of three chickens. They are named for their looks. You know…"

"Yes I know, and WE are not the proud owners of any such things as chickens, unless WE are going to eat them tomorrow. Where in God's name did they come from?" She stood a good ten feet away. "Get that dirty box out of here. Animals do not belong on the kitchen table unless they are on a plate."

Ike ignored her and lifted out a tiny ball of fuzz with, yes, a naked neck. It blinked once and settled into the curve of his hand. He scooped out another. The box started peeping. The next thing Julia knew there were three very odd looking birds on her kitchen floor. They huddled together, gave a shiver, and pooped in unison.

"I'll take care of them. Oh Mother, please, please let me. We are starting a club at school. We're going to call it the 'The Boys' Pecker Neck Club'. James gave them to us and he said they are easy to keep. Oh, please, Mother, please." Julia slowly sank down onto the pantry step stool. She stared at the chicks. She'd seen the breed before. Her mama'd kept a small spot for chickens out back by the stream. They were mostly fat broodies, but somewhere along the line, a few pecker necks had been added to the mix. Mama called the rooster Cletus. Flossie Mae remembered the day when they ate him. The meat was tough.

Julia gave her son 'The Look'. "Get the floor mop; you have a job to do, and where do you propose to house those animals? We are not farmers, you know."

Young Ike was ready for that one. The boys rehearsed their defense before they left the schoolyard. "I can build a wire pen out by the shed. When they get old enough, I'll build nesting boxes. James knows all about it. He said he'd help us."

"Why is James doing this? Did his mother say he was allowed to hand out chickens at school?"

"Oh, yes ma'am. He said his mother would let him keep two and to get rid of the rest. So he did."

"I'm not surprised." Julia knew Flora Williams would not be wasting her time or feed money with a lot of fancy chickens. Pecker necks laid small eggs, if she remembered correctly. Leghorns are a much better hen to have. She sat, watching the fluff balls on the floor. You must admit they were cute for an oddity. Ike never even so much as brought home a stray cat before. She stood up and approached the menagerie.

"Son, please put them back in the box and set it out on the stoop. Get one of the old sauce dishes and give them some water. There is stale bread in the box. Then mop this floor. We'll discuss this with your father this evening."

"Yes, Mother. Uh, does this mean you like them?"

"Son, this means I love you." With a hug and kiss, she left the beaming boy to his chores. Julia went to the parlor and waited for her husband. She remembered standing with her mama, scattering whatever they had for garbage around those chickens by the stream. It was fun to watch them scrabble and squawk over the leftover scraps. Ike came home to a smiling wife. The cage was built that evening.

The chicks were named Patty, Pullet, and Peter Pecker Neck. Julia never once said their last names, but for some reason, her two Ikes thought it was hilarious. They would look at each other and howl. They never missed a chance to call them by their full names. Then one day she realized what they were saying. They were all out back and both Ikes were standing by the pen, tossing cracked corn through the wire mesh.

"You two will not, I repeat, not say the chickens' last name again. I will not have dirty talk in this house." Julia's face was a bright pink. She'd been sweeping the stoop when she realized the name joke. Raising the broom handle like a sword, she stomped across the yard toward the shed. She was furious. Ike senior looked her straight in the eye.

"My good wife, we are not in the house, we are in the yard. Only the ground is dirty out here." She swung the broom at him, missing by a mile. "I suggest you not even try to sweep the yard, it's far too dusty." He smiled at her and looked down at his son. "Should we promise Mother to watch our chicken talk in the house? I think she's not very happy with us. We shouldn't egg her on."

This time the broom landed full force on Ike's seat. That swat sealed the deal. "We promise. No more pecker neck talk in front of any lady. Son, shall we leave the P.N. family to their corn? It looks like they are pecking away." Ike grabbed the broom before she gave it another swing.

The three walked back to the house, smiling. "You two are lucky we aren't having chicken and dumplings for supper."

Julia didn't want to think any more about chickens. Those creatures belonged on a farm and she didn't. She worked too hard and come too far. She insisted Ikey do all chicken keeping, which included the pen cleaning. Surprisingly enough, he was good at it. She never smelled the droppings. Come to think of it, she never saw them, either.

"Son, when you clean the pen, what do you do with the, you know?" Mother and child were at the kitchen table, finishing Saturday dinner. Julia wasn't about to get into a poop discussion, but she was curious. She was proud of how well he was doing with his chores. "I never smell anything nasty."

The boy looked up from his tapioca, a favorite desert, and grinned. "I sell it." A big spoonful of pudding entered his mouth.

"You what?" she choked. Her coffee was poised in her hand. Thank goodness she hadn't had a drink yet.

"The Boys Pecker Neck Club sells poop."

"Watch it, young man. To who?" She was more than curious.

"Ladies like poop." He was having fun with this one. Another scoop of tapioca found its mark.

"Not another bite until you tell me what is going on." Julia set down her cup and took the bowl away from him. Ikey slowly rolled the cream covered pearls around his mouth, savoring his mother's reaction just as much as the sweetness. After a dramatic swallow, he spoke.

"Did you know that some neighbor ladies use chicken sh, uh puh, uh droppings on their flowers?"

"No." She really did, but didn't let on. Her mama used to do that, mixing hay and poop until it was hot. Then she'd put it on the garden.

"They let the mess get old in a bucket," said Ikey.

"Then they put lots of water over it and let it soak for a week. They call it chicken tea. When it's ready, the ladies dipper the tea over their flowers. What do you think of that?"

Julia touched the corner of her mouth, indicating to Ikey to use his napkin. "I think you are a business man," she said. "Does your father know?"

"No. Should I tell him?"

"Oh yes. He would be proud of you."

"I'll do it tonight," and he did. Ike set up an accounting system for his son, insisting he save twenty percent. The rest was for him to use as he wanted. Ikey quickly upped the ante when he played marbles, knowing his return. He called it investing.

One sunny morning when Ikey went out back to check the water supply in the pen, he saw an egg out in the open. He raced back to the house, grabbed his mother's hand, pulling her out to the cage. "Look, look. We have eggs."

"Get James over here. We need nesting boxes. Your chicks are officially grown up." She stood by her son and held her arm straight out to her side. Oh my, he was as tall as her armpit. When did her chick go? "Not yet, not yet."

"What, Mother?"

"Oh nothing. I'm just seeing how tall you are." She gave him a smile and a hug. Julia turned, walking to the house. "Make sure James teaches you how to make the box," she called before she let the screen door slam. "Not yet, my baby," she whispered to herself.

***

Nesting boxes were built. It seemed all the boys had eggs show up just about the same time. At the next club meeting, held under the big tree out by the ditch next to where the girls always sat at school recess, the boys were full of egg talk.

"I got sooo many eggs that my mama wants to sell

them. I told her 'no way, no how'. Those are my eggs."
Richard owned four chicks.

"We're getting' so rich sellin' shit, why not sell
eggs." James' language could be as ripe as their tea.
"Who's got a butt load of eggs? I bet I got more 'en you."
The entire club agreed to bring their bounty to school the
next day. Whoever had the most would win the bet, get to
sell them all, and keep the money. The boys concluded with
their private handshake: three flaps of their wings, two
pecks of their heads, and a squat of their bottoms. None of
them realized they weren't actually shaking hands at all.
They just knew their club was the best in the world.

The next day's recess found four boys under the
tree with pasteboard boxes. From a distance it looked like a
church picnic, not a meeting of a secret society. They were
sitting in a circle with their lidded containers in front of
them. Each was hoping they had the most. There would be
the big payoff.

"Ready. At the count of three, lids off." Ikey hoped
he would win. "One, two, three." Off came the lids.

"AWWW," they cried in unison. Each boy had two
eggs, a four way tie.

"That ain't enough to sell. What are we going to
do?" Christopher, James' cousin, had his hopes set on the
money 'cause his mama never had any for 'that truck', the
penny candy sticks Christopher loved. Richard stood up
with his box. Holding it close, he looked both ways. Not a
grown-up in sight. He flipped the lid open and grabbed an
egg.

"EEEHOW. Injuns." He spun and threw, hitting
Ikey square in the chest. "WAR."

Ten seconds later The Boys Pecker Neck Club was
rolling on the ground, covered with slime and dust,
pounding on each other. The girls were screaming and the
principal materialized out of nowhere. He stood there with
his arms folded in front of him, letting them go at it for

what seemed like forever to the girls. Milly Williams, James' sister tugged on the principal's sleeve.

"You gonna stop them?" she asked.

"In a bit. They need to wear themselves out first. You girls step back, don't want you all hurt, too." After about thirty more seconds, he put two fingers in his mouth and blew the whistle every student knew meant "You. Listen." Sure enough, the war ended as quickly as it began. The boys stood up, looked at themselves, and started giggling. They were wearing their profit.

"Gentlemen, are you quite through? I think you have provided entertainment enough for one day." The principal turned to the girls who were laughing as much as the boys. Shaking his head, he said, "Ladies, may I present your future husbands. God save us all." Turning back to the warriors, he said, "This meeting is closed. Go see what you can do at the pump before you come back in. Your mothers can deal with you later. Ladies, off you go, your lessons are waiting." As soon as the principal and the girls headed toward the building, the boys circled and did their handshake, working very hard but not succeeding in keeping their faces serious. The last part, the egg-laying squat, landed them all on the ground again, howling. It was a good fifteen minutes before The Boys' Pecker Neck Club was presentable enough to enter class.

Two weeks later disaster struck the Jameson chicken pen. The family heard the squawks and screams. Julia knew the sound, but couldn't tell her men. Sure enough, all three chickens were dead, their heads gone, a sure sign of raccoon. Ike wouldn't let Ikey see. Julia held her sobbing son while the animals were boxed and a grave was prepared in the far corner of the yard. No one even suggested eating them. When the site was ready, Ike called for his family. Patty, Pullet and Peter were laid to rest with Julia reading Matthew 23 verse 37, the only Bible reference to chickens she could find. Ikey only ate vegetables for several days afterwards in honor of the deceased. Very soon, the rest of the club gave up the chicken business and let their mothers do as they wished with the lot. Not one family had pecker neck stew, thanks to the pleading of the boys. Their pets were sold and the money was split four ways, even though Ikey had none to contribute. The Boys' Pecker Neck Club stayed true blue 'til the end…or at least until they discovered girls.

Chapter 22

THE CANARY

"Is she is, or is she ain't?" Jack was twitchin' a jig with Sure Foot avoiding the high kicking. "Is she is, or is she ain't your sweetheart?" The young men were busy in the hold. The last off load was the spices, and the heat and the fumes in the bottom of the boat was enough to make an old man choke. The two buddies always got the stink assignments because their lungs could take it, and after all, they both got their start in the bilge.

"Quit kickin', start workin." Sure Foot did not want teasin' today. There was something on his mind Jack did not know about. This something could make or break their partnership. Jack just grinned and wiggled his shoulders in the same dance way.

"Yes, suh." Jack would break into slave talk when he wanted Sure Foot to quit his bossing. "I's be doin' yo work fo ya. You jist watch." With that, Jack clicked his heels and made a hat sweeping bow. He picked up a hefty burlap bag of vanilla beans and dropped it into the barrow. Sure Foot followed with his. They stopped and assessed their work. They had twenty-four thousand pounds to move that day, and dancin' didn't get it done. As soon as one barrow was full, they wheeled it over to the lift pallet and arranged the load for the men up top. Four trips with a barrow and Jack pulled the bell rope. The pallet rose, only to be returned, hungry for more. They worked hard, stopping only for mess. The team finished the last in the dark. Sure Foot knew he had to make his say. He sat on the allspice berries, their assignment for tomorrow.

"You good with your silver?" Sure Foot could see Jack's eyes and that was about all.

"Uh huh." Those eyes moved in a nod.

"I held something back."

"Hmmm."

"You remember the yellow diamond and the cameo?"

"Damn it man, what are you getting at?" Jack was losing his patience. His hammock was calling his name after this long, hot day.

"I owe you for those pieces. I never gave 'em to Flossie for sellin' and I need to get square with you about it." Sure Foot's guilt was rising in his voice. "I think I want Missus Myra to have them. You know, as a present. From me. If she will take them." His words were rushing now. "She's one fine woman. I want her have something to help her think about me." His words were done.

"Two five dollar silver and we'll call it even." Jack was grinning. He was right. Sure Foot had a sweetheart. He fell asleep that night thinking about the redheaded fish gal. Maybe someday he could give her a pretty little something. Sure Foot didn't sleep at all. They would be sailing soon and he had to get his courage up enough to show his heart.

Myra was late on the wharves the next day. Just because her children were old enough to go to school did not guarantee their arrival at the front gate. More than once Junior had been called into the office to give some guidance as to where the other four'd gone off to. Junior knew their usual spots, but was sick and tired of chasing them. So today he shrugged and said "Ask Mama."

The principal nodded. Mr. Dirkman and Junior had an understanding. He knew when the boy wasn't talking, he was fed up. Who wouldn't be? Junior Gallaway worked harder at raising his sister and brothers than any eleven year old had a right to. As the child passed by the school's secretary, she handed him an anise ball. He popped it in his mouth and tucked it deep in his cheek. There it stayed for an hour as he sat doing his lessons. The licorice flavor soothed him. Biting the tiny seed in the center was always a fine way to end arithmetic.

Myra was just finishing arranging her wares when her front bell rang.

"Mrs. Gallaway? It's Principal Dirkman. Are you home?"

Myra spoke through the screen. "Who's hurt?"

"Your youngest four are gone missing. Junior said to ask you. I think he's looking for a break."

Myra tied on her black bonnet, grabbed up the loaded basket, and stepped out on the porch. She latched the door and pushed the screen shut. She knew Junior wanted a break and did not have to have this man tellin' her so. Shoot, *she* needed a break. Myra adjusted her load and looked up at the Principal.

"Let's go toward the store. Sometimes they can trick my uncle into thinkin' it's a day off." Harry always kept rice and beans stewing in the back. Any hungry man coming to the side door could have a meal, just for the asking. To treat the little ones he would dish out a plate of rice, pour some sweet molasses over it, and the children would be in heaven. Myra knew Aunt Ada would have shooed them off to school by now, so today must be Guild. If they were at the store, Uncle Harry would have his hands full. She stepped up her pace.

Mr. Dirkman was giving her the what-for. Ever since Benjy went to jail, the school people had it in their mind that Myra should be spending more time at home. One do-gooder even had the gall to suggest she should start going to church on Wednesday where she might have more of a chance to meet a respectable man to marry. Then she would be a better mother. How was she going to be a better mother with another belly full of baby? That's what Myra wanted to know.

"Mr. Dirkman, thank you for your advice. Just as soon as we find these children, I will stop all my hard working at feeding, housing and clothing them, hire me a colored girl, and become the fine mother you expect me to be. Perhaps you would like to pay my bills? Oh, right, if you did that, I would be your wife. Frankly sir, I do think Mrs. Dirkman would object, and if you think I will become anyone's totsy, you are sadly mistaken." The set on Myra's chin warned the man to keep his mouth shut for the rest of the trip.

Myra flung open the store's front door. "Benjy, Franky, Theo, Nora Lee, get your bottoms out here. Hello, Uncle Harry. Principal Dirkman's chasing children. You have any?"

"Darlin'. Brother." Harry acknowledged them both and tilted his head toward the back of the store. Sitting on the floor like so many Indians were her children. Each with a dish, sticky brown lips, and a guilty look. The boys'd been in school long enough to know what was coming next. There was a paddle waiting for them in the principal's office. Franky began to cough and sniffle. Benjy elbowed him. Theo picked rice from his front teeth. Nora Lee kept licking her plate, ignoring the whole situation.

"What brings you two here on the children's day off?"

"No day off. Playing hookie." Myra reached behind the counter for the wooden yardstick. She turned to Principal Dirkman. "I will take care of the beatin', if you don't mind. I do know how important my mothering ways are to you." Her tone said it all. The men looked at each other and stepped back.

"Each of you will go wash your face in the basin by the necessary. If you take too long I will give you more than you've asked for. While you are cleaning up, figure how you are going to apologize to Uncle Harry for tricking him."

Nora Lee looked up from her plate. "Mama, I'm bein-havin'."

"Scoot."

Each child got as many swats as they were old.

When it was done and they spoke to their great uncle, she dismissed the children and the Principal with "Now go!" Mr. Dirkman and the four children practically ran out of the door, tails tucked. She turned to Uncle Harry. "You got any coffee with that rice?" The two sat with their own plates, talking weather and young'uns. Then Myra kissed her uncle's cheek with her own sticky lips, washed herself up and headed on down to the docks, basket on her arm.

The *Sallie Lou* was a'fixin' to sail tomorrow. She really did enjoy talking to Sure Foot. The recent adventures raised her appreciation of the man. Today would be their last visit for weeks to come.

"Oh sailor man, oh sailor man." Her call brought him running down the plank. The wharf was not busy as many ships were finishing their last load and most hands were busy securing the holds. Sure Foot found himself facing Myra alone. He breathed deep. *Now or never, here I go.*

"Missus Myra."

"Yes?"

"I have to tell you something."

"Oh my, is Jack hurt again?"

"No. Nothing like that. It's just we're sailing tomorrow and I have to tell you something."

She looked him straight in the eye. "So tell."

"You are so nice and pretty."

"Pshaw. You need spectacles." She grinned at him.

"I think you are the nicest woman I have ever met. I like you, and you're short." The words did not surprise her. She'd seen it in his eyes a while back. Her face went serious.

"I like you, and you're short, too." They both laughed.

"Oh, Myra, I don't want you to forget me."

"Goodness, I can't do that. You and I see eye to eye."

"Would you take something to remember me by? It's what I really want you to have."

"Of course, but I wouldn't forget you anyway." Myra reddened.

"Might I send you a letter when I'm out to sea? Postal boats sail regular from Havana. That is, if you don't mind." Sure Foot didn't know he could be so forward, but here he was, ready to make the step. He reached into his pocket and handed her a wadded up handkerchief. "Don't look now. You don't have to wear either of them if you don't want to, but please don't give them away." She quickly dropped the bulky cloth into her apron pocket.

"You do realize I have five children, don't you?"

"Yes ma'am, I do."

"I am older than you."

"Makes sense with five young'uns."

They started walking away in opposite directions. Myra turned.

"How are you going to write me when you don't even know where to send it?" She was smiling that wonderful smile of hers.

"Hadn't thought that far. Where?"

"I live at 23 Drury Lane. You know, just like the Muffin Man song."

Later that night, after supper and good night prayers, Myra sat alone at her kitchen table. She opened the handkerchief and stared. There was a finely made cameo. The lady on the brooch had been carved so that there was a blush of pink just at her throat. She was beautiful. Then her eye looked beyond the lady. Rumpled in the cloth, she saw a thin gold band. She pulled it free and burst into tears. In her hand was a woman's ring. The stone was the color of yellow fire. Sure Foot had given her a diamond the size she'd never seen before in her life. She slipped it on her hand and held it out to catch the light of her kitchen lantern. It shone the color of gold, of the sun, of a canary.

The dream was so real that when she woke up the next morning, she felt it was true. CB Ledbetter was sittin' at a kitchen table, not one she ever knew, and was listening to the children doing sums. They were calling him 'Daddy CB' like it was their life. It looked like CB had gone from nothin' to husband in a blink. *My dear Jesus*, she thought, *there really is something to all this.* "Oh Everett, I don't remember what it was like," Myra said out loud to that distant ghost. She'd been married when she was thirteen with a baby on the way, a life-time ago. Now she was a woman, a mother with more responsibilities than any one person should have. Did the dream mean she was might be ready to try again? His gifts certainly implied he liked her. He said as much. He did make her happy every time they saw each other on the docks. She was dressed and out the door before she even realized it.

The *Sallie* was still in her slip, but not for long. All the men were at their workstations, preparations for departure were in their final phases.

"Sure Foot, Sure Foot Ledbetter, where are you?" Myra stood at the gangplank yelling louder than she ever called out before. "Men, where is Sure Foot? I must ask him something."

Jack leaned over the side. "He's with Cookie. I'll get him. Everyone good with you?"

"Yes. Thank you. Please hurry." Jack disappeared.

Within a blink or two, Sure Foot was at the top of the plank. "I can't come down, we're soon gone. Are you all safe? What has happened?"

Myra drew a breath. "I just need to know something. Are you courting me?"

"Yes, I think so. Uh, uh, yes, I know so."

"Good. I will look forward to that."

The first packet of letters arrived soon after. After reading, she tied a red hair ribbon around them.

Hello. I hope you are fine. I am fine and busy. Thank you for letting me write to you. Sincerely, CB (Sure Foot)

#

Dear Myra. We are on our way south. Black Jack and I are working hard. Not to brag, but we are a good team and our work gets done right on time. That's how come I can write you. CB

#

Dear Myra. Today I spent most of the time with the Captain. He is a real good man. I help him with the charts and things like that. I am learning things. The Captain likes to tell me sea stories. I get to borrow his books. CB PS. We are in Havana. I will post these now.

#

Dear Myra. I forgot to ask about the children. I hope they are not troubling you too much. Today Jack and I sang a new song we learned from his book. I don't think you have ever heard us sing since we do it in the taverns and I know you would never go to any place like that.

Maybe we could sing for you when we get back. I would like to do it for you. CB

#

Dear Myra. We are almost to Panama. Had some rough weather and couldn't write, but things are smooth, now. I will post this when we dock. I don't know if you will get it. I hope. I miss seeing you. You are so pretty. I hope you liked your presents.

Give Flossie my love. Can I say the same to you? CB

Chapter 23

PROPER PROPERTY

After the initial jewelry sale to the church ladies, Julia needed to be more careful. It would make no sense to have an unending supply of family things to sell. It startled her, however, to see one of the sets in the Goldstein's display window. It was the coral cameo, ear bobs and negligee pendant she had sold to Justine Richardson, one of the newest members of the guild. Julia entered to shop. Mrs. Hilda Goldstein was working behind the counter.

"Good morning, Missus uh, uh." It was evident Marty's Mama did not know her from Eve. That was good.

"Good morning, Mrs. Goldstein. Isn't a sunny day? I noticed how nice things looked in your front window. That beautiful necklace set caught my eye."

"Would you like to see it? It's coral color certainly would look good with your complexion. Let me get it out for you."

"What are you asking for the set?"

When told the price, Julia caught her breath. Marty Mark-up had done his job. "Oh, Mrs. Goldstein, I wish I could buy it. It is so beautiful. However, my situation in life has taken a turn. The real reason I am here is I need to sell." Julia went into the tale of her wedding gifts from heaven, her hardworking husband, and her need to save his pride. Mrs. Goldstein'd heard it all before and figured she had an easy buy. Julia spent the next few months dealing with Hilda.

Very soon they both realized no one could have so many 'wedding gifts' and the women dropped the ruse. Julia came home with a lesser profit for all, but the safety of the exchange and the ease of handling the silver certificate bills was worth it. Both women knew the benefits outweighed the truth. Hilda never told Julia that several of the pieces she brought in had their origins from that very shop. She just bought them back without comment. Some she re-sold outright. The ones she felt might draw attention she gave to her darling son, Marty. He removed the stones and rendered the metal. A diamond and ruby pendant became two different rings. Many of the unsellables became unrecognizable. Marty designed and cast the new jewelry with a flare few men possessed. The mother-son team flourished with the pieces created from Julia's visits.

There was almost a kinship between the two women as they did business. They chatted as they did their exchange, realizing they'd some things in common. They both loved their sons, and after all, Hilda Goldstein had been married to a man who liked numbers, too.

Julia loved the shopping. It started soon after she replaced the dining room carpet and realized Ike hadn't noticed.

"If that man is so blind he can't see a new rug right under his feet, well then, let's see if he sees something right under his nose." Julia bought new men's handkerchiefs and had them monogramed with Ike's initials. She even ordered a set of small ones for her son, marked the same. Neither Ike noticed the newness as she handed each a fresh one, initials side up, as they dressed for church. Both just shoved their handkerchief in their pocket, picked up their Bibles and waited for her on the porch.

"Like father, like son," she smiled as she passed by them, letting the screen door scrape shut. As they walked to services, Julia planned to thank God for her ignorant men. If this was any indication of their lack of attention to detail, maybe she could buy a new table cloth. Later on she did that just that. She proudly served Sunday dinner on the linen, using the matching napkins. No one noticed.

Ike never saw the clothing. Julia knew if she

showed up at the table in new finery, his accounting head would explode. She waved farewell to and met her family in the evening wearing her everyday dresses. She wore her everyday shoes. She kept her everyday cape and hat hanging on the coat tree in the entry. Every day, as soon as they were on their way, she changed. The jewelry business allowed her to buy what she was not allowed to have. Shoes matched dresses matched hats matched outer wear. She hid all the clothing on a second rack behind Young Ike's church shirts. He was still in knickers, so there was extra space in the wardrobe. The shoes and reticules were tucked in the back right-hand corner in an old box. The new hat boxes were stacked in the corner of the kitchen pantry, covered with the faded tablecloth.

Today the hens would see the periwinkle dress with those beautiful blue shoes. She was deciding if this or the gray and purple one with the striped pumps was her favorite when someone pulled her front bell. Still in her housedress, she answered the door.

There stood Black Jack, looking like a raggedy man.

"Ma'am, I's lookin' fo' day work. It'd be mighty kin' if you'd hiuh me fer tha day."

"Get to the back," she snapped. "You know better." She slammed the door.

She let him into the kitchen with her hands on her hips.

"What do you mean by ringing my bell? You know colored can't come in the front, and what's this about day work? CB told me you learned straight talk from him. You don't need to be 'hiud fer tha day'." She was giving him the Mama look, but did not realize he didn't know the what-was-what about that. "Why are you dressed that way? You are not common." She nodded to the kitchen chair.

"I'll bet Sure Foot thinks of his mama when he talks to you." Jack sat down, wondering if Sure Foot called her

Bossy Flossie when they were little. All the slave talk was gone. "I had to be low nigger in case neighbors were watching. Sure Foot thinks me doing yard work for you would be safer than him coming around and getting noticed. You favor each other, you know."

"What's going on? Does he need me?"

"We've got a trading problem, and he can't tell Missus Myra about it."

"You stay in here about thirty seconds more and then we'll both have more than a trading problem. Let's go out to the garden and get you to work. Tell me then. It'll look like I'm supervising new help."

Julia showed Jack the tool shed. He got the hoe, rake, and spade. She took him to the former location of the chicken scratch.

"I need a garden cut. Ikey used to have chickens here, so it's bare anyway. Are you sure you can do it?" She winked.

"I's de bes' garden cuttin' man der is. I cuts good fo' you, 'specially dis late in da summer."

She had no idea what she would do with another garden, but her feeling of adventure was rising again. She stood close. "Talk."

"Sure Foot and I made a trade the other night we know we can't do anything with."

"Really? We've been handling the jewelry just fine. What did you take this time that you can't keep?"

"Ma'am, you's got yo'self one fine house. I sees dat fo' a fact."

Julia startled. "What?"

"Dis is one fin' house. Dat's what I's talkin' about."

"Speak white. No one is out here but us." She walked a few paces away from where he was breaking ground and pointed. "Cut to here."

"We took a deed. We are now the owners of a house on the mainland."

"Oh, God in heaven, what were you two thinking? You suppose Myra and I can sell a house like so many ear bobs? You two are plum crazy. Keep digging."

"We don't want it sold. We need to know what it is worth." Jack slowed his digging.

"Why? Are you going into the real estate business?"

"Your brother wants to own it, free and clear. He wants to buy my half."

Julia stood there, staring. "What in heaven's name does he need with a house?"

Jack started hoeing the clods he had turned.

"That man thinks a house is a good thing to hold a family."

"What fam…ohhhh, do you mean a family with lots of children?"

Jack smiled. "Yes, ma'am." He kept his eyes on the dirt.

"Does Myra know?"

"Gawd, no. He is not stepping up until things are in place. He's askin' you to keep his secret." Jack stopped the hoeing and looked Julia straight in the eye. No colored man had ever done that to her before. She looked away.

"Watch your manners with me. Anything in the neighborhood can cause talk. Keep your eyes down."

""Yez ma'am. I do's it, ma'am." He broke another clod. "Can you help your brother? I brought the deed with me so's you can find out about it."

"You tell that fool he has no brains whatsoever. You also tell him I love him. I'll do what I can, and, yes, I'll keep his secret."

Jack left the deed in the shed when he put away the tools. Out front, she loudly told him to come back later. She must leave soon, and she would not have work done without her watching. She'd get word to him to finish the garden when she could be there and she would pay him when the job was done. Jack kept nodding and winking as he backed down to the street. Julia retrieved the deed in its brown envelope and hid it in her glove drawer. Oh, dear lord, what'd she gotten herself into?

She changed her mind about her clothing and put on the purple and gray set. She only worn it one time before, and felt there'd been enough time passed to show it off again. She loved the color combination and felt like she looked rich. Julia always wanted to make an impression on the hens. As she walked to the church, she planned.

"I'm going to have to go to some bank where they don't know me and ask about the deed. The banker will think I'm straight up if I dress just right," Julia thought to herself. She decided to go to the City National Bank. It was across town, and the people wouldn't know her from nothing. "I'll claim the deed's an unexpected inheritance and I need to know all about the property." She smiled to herself. This was going to be the most exciting thing yet. With a quick check of her face in a storefront glass, she walked into the church. This kind of secret keeping was fun.

***

After the *Sallie* sailed long enough to ensure the original land owner was long gone, Julia gussied up in the purple and gray combination again. It was hotter than the dickens and she was afraid her starch would wilt, but what could she do? Ike was too cheap to own a horse and carriage, and hiring a hack would draw attention to the house. So off she went, walking in those beautiful shoes.

"I am an idiot." Her monthly was due any day and her back was aching. No matter, she kept on walking. "I am a blessed idiot." She talked herself all the way to the middle of town. Then she started thinking through her plan. The deed was in her reticule. She was an heiress, a fuddle-headed heiress. Could they please check the value of the property? She entered the bank. The bank clerk told Julia to go to the court house for the information.

"Oh, sir, I just don't know what to do. Are you sure there is no way this bank can help me?" Julia stood, twisting her handkerchief.

"All right, I'll speak to the manager, Mr. Nash. Please be seated, Mrs. Uh, Uh?"

"Shipper. Mrs. Jack Shipper. My friends call me by my given name, Sallie Lou."

"Mrs. Shipper, may I show the deed to Mr. Nash? I am hoping he can help."

"Of course." Julia fumbled in her bag and handed him the deed. The clerk opened the envelope.

"Tell me again, who is John Parsons?" The clerk seemed far too interested in the document for Julia's comfort.

"I will be glad to discuss my family linage with your manager." The clerk got the Mama stare. The young man knew exactly what it meant.

"Excuse me, ma'am. I'll be right back."

Oh, dear Lord, that was close. Sallie Lou Shipper, for God's sake, and just who is John Parsons? I'm guessing the name on the deed. By the time this day is over, I will be on the path to Perdition. Julia was deep in thought when the manager invited her into his office. She listened as the manager repeated the clerk's information about the court house. Julia took out her handkerchief.

"I was shocked, sir, to receive this document. My parents, God rest their souls, never once spoke of kin." Sniff. Dab. "I can only guess Mr. John Parsons was from my mother's side. When she eloped with Daddy, her people cut her off. She used to speak of her Uncle John, though. I never knew his last name." Sob. "Please, could you check this property? I never thought there was anyone left." Sniff, sob. "What a joy it would be to know there was family who cared." Boo, hoo, hoo.

It worked. Mr. Nash sent one of the mortgage clerks to do the research. After a very nervous while a packet

161

addressed to 'Mrs. Shipper' was handed over with well wishes concerning her new inheritance. Julia was soon on her way home. She skittered in the front door with only minutes to change clothes. She hid the envelope in her Sunday coat and was cooking supper when the family arrived. The two men in her life were off to practice their evening numbers when Julia finally got a chance to look in the envelope. There was the deed and a value description letter.

It was quite a while before she came out of their room. Her brother owned an eight room house in La Porte. There was running water in the kitchen, a screened sleeping porch, and one of the rooms had privy plumbing.

Oh, Mama, look at us, look at your babies. Please Mama, be proud. Julia could only hope.

Jack fetched the deed from the shed when he came to finish the garden and tucked it in his shirt. So much time passed since the initial cut, the square was one big weed patch. Julia felt any more work would be fruitless and made a big show of getting rid of Jack. She winked and ran him off with a hoe.

On ship Jack handed his best friend the packet. Sure Foot was singing the nursery rhyme about the Muffin Man. He'd changed the words.

"Do you know the Muffin Gal, the Muffin Gal, the "Muffin Gal?

"Do you know the Muffin Gal who lives on Drury Lane?

"Yes I know…"

"Lordy man, open the envelope." Jack was tapping his foot, and it wasn't to the beat of the song. "What we got?"

Sure Foot read the value statement twice.

"Oh man, oh man, oh man. It's gonna be sometime before I can pay you off. Look at this thing."

Jack took the document and grinned. "You be a po'

man in a rich man's house, that fo' sure."

"I'll pay you every cent. You know I will."

"I know it. You're gonna be one fine daddy someday to those young'uns. When are you going to propose to Missus Myra? After all, what if she says 'No'? Then you'd be in the pickle barrel, for sure."

"I think next time we come in. Still gotta make some money to give you first." Sure Foot folded the deed and put it back in the envelope.

"Don't you wait too long. Y'all don't know what the future'll bring."

"Mebe I should write her a letter."

"Mebe you should," Jack agreed. "What else ya got to do between here and Panama, grow a garden?"

Dear Myra. I have something to talk to you about. I really want to see you soon. It's important. CB

\#

Dear Myra. Jack says I should tell you what happened. I can't believe that it's true. I hope you will like my news. I can't wait to tell you. I like you so much. CB

\#

Dear Myra. My last letter said that I liked you. That was a lie. I love you. CB

\#

Dear Myra. I hope you are not mad at me for saying I love you. I really do. Could you ever feel the same way for me? I know I am short and ugly. Can someone as pretty as you see past that?

I hope so because I want to tell you something and ask you something. With love, CB Ledbetter

Chapter 24

JARRED PEACHES

Myra could smell it. There was something different about the docks this early mornin'. It was almost fall, so it wasn't a change of the fish sour. That happened in December when temperature was down. She didn't notice it in the counting house. She had brought Mr. Jameson his usual treats, but he wasn't at his desk. She asked the men where he was because she wanted to make sure he got his favorites. After all, Ike Jameson was the one who let her walk as freely as she did.

"Mr. Jameson is in town on very special business." Mr. Thomas always loved to show his own importance.

"What business is that?" Myra gave Mr. Thomas a wink, making him blush to his collar.

"Why, this Saturday morning, September 8, 1900, our boss is receiving an award for the tight accounting we do. He has taken Young Ike with him to the Tremont House for the day's meal and events. He wants the boy to see what rewards there are in counting. This is one proud day for the whole office." Mr. Thomas was bragging like he was the boss.

Myra smiled. If there was ever going to be someone good with counting, it would be Young Ike. He finally collected his nickel bet from Junior with the skin of his knuckles. Junior learned after the dust-up not to wager unless it was a sure thing. He also learned never to make Ikey a money bet at marbles again. He'd play Picking Plums, but that's all. Sometimes he'd win, sometimes he'd lose, but he always kept his best plums in his pocket, tied up in the cloth sack Aunt Ada sewed for him with scraps from an old apron.

"Well, Mr. Thomas, if it's all right with you, I am going to leave some plunkets on his desk. If he doesn't come back today, you make sure the package is taken care of. They might go stale by Monday. We can't let that happen, now can we?" She grinned broadly and so did Mr. Thomas. The young man knew he and his mama would be having dessert tonight.

Myra walked through the counting house, smiling and joking. With no one to stop the men from buying right there in the office, Missus Gallaway's apron pockets were jingling before she put one foot on the dock. A dozen steps outside and she stopped. The smell was wrong. The sun was shining off to the north. Even though there was the usual morning light rain, the sea was not calm. She walked to the first slip. That ship rocked, scraping on the wood. Ships at berth don't move like that. She called her wares.

"Oh sailor man, oh sailor man, sweet things are in my basket. Come down and see, come down and see, sweet things are in my basket." She was soon surrounded, smiling, chatting, and selling. She thought about Sure Foot.

"Anyone here see the *Sallie Lou*?"

"She'd be by Panama 'bout now," came the reply.

Myra nodded, thanked the man, and continued along the dock. What was that she smelled? What made the berthed ships rock? She stopped stock still. Whatever it was, it was bad. That was the smell she knew from the day her husband died. She smelled doom.

Oh, dear Jesus, she thought. *I have got to get home, now. Something is happening. I have got to find the children. I have got to go to Aunt Ada and Uncle Harry. Oh, dear God, I have to move, now.* She spun around and practically ran back to the counting house. She stopped, catching her breath. She knew Mr. Thomas would get all flustered if he saw her running. She opened the door, nodded to the men as she walked through the opening between the rows of desks and calmly exited, shutting the door behind. Then she did start to run. The smell was stronger than ever. She ran as though the Devil was on her tail. She didn't know why, but she knew.

The grocery was closer to the wharves than The Shoe. She burst through the shop door. Myra stopped, breathed deeply, and looked around. Uncle Harry must be somewhere in the back. Sulee was behind the counter with her feather duster. You had to admit the stock never been so clean since Sulee came to work. She dusted the duster handle when she thought no one was looking, bless her heart.

"Miss Sulee?" The girl looked up and smiled.

"Yes'm? How are you, Missus Myra?"

"Where is Uncle Harry?" Myra had no time for pleasantries with the shop girl.

"Out back, feeding the rats." Sulee always wished the rot dump was farther away from the back door, but she was too shy to ask to have it moved. She just called it the rat house, hoping Mr. Harry would get the message. He never listened to Sulee about anything, so the comments concerning the growing rodent population went unheeded, too.

Feigning calm, Myra walked through the store and out the back. She hated the dump, too, but knew why it was there. Uncle Harry loved to sit with his rifle on an upturned crate by the edge of that nasty trash pile and take target practice. Sure enough, there he was. He'd brought out another crate and set a mug of chicory coffee and his chewed up, nasty cigar butt on it. It looked like a tea party for old men. Today he was sitting there in his slicker.

"What's your number today?"

"Four kill, two wing. Darlin', what are you doing here? Hidin' from the young'uns?"

She walked over to the crates, pecked him on the cheek, picked up his coffee cup and took a taste. She knew he'd have a bit of really bad whiskey in it. She took a full swallow and handed him the cigar. She sat on the crate beside him.

"Uncle Harry, your coffee's so strong you could give it a job."

He smiled, and loaded the .22 for another round at the rats.

"Uncle Harry, do you remember when the cholera hit Everett?"

"Of course I do." He took a full look at her for the first time since she sat down. "Child, why do you ask? Is something wrong?" He stared at her, noticing how flushed she was.

"Uncle Harry, I smell it. I smelled it on the docks. I smell it here."

He chuckled. "Child, this is a rot dump. Of course it smells."

"No, Uncle Harry, I'm serious. I smell the same thing I smelled when Everett died. I smell doom." She put down his cup and grabbed his hands. She rushed on. "I don't know what it is, but it's here. The ships at the dock are shifting. The wind is wrong. My entire soul feels scared, really scared."

He looked at her hard. "Child, what do you need?"

"We have to go home. We have to get Aunt Ada. We have to find the children." She started to gasp. "Uncle Harry, we have to go now. Please close the store for dinner and come with me."

Harry slowly stood up, rifle in hand, and turned to Myra. The sky was clouding and he noticed Myra did not have her rain cape. He saw the fear in her eyes. He smelled rot and nothing else, but he did know the look of fear. "It's only about ten o'clock, but I'll send Miss Sulee home and head on to the church for your Aunt Ada. You herd up your children and we'll meet you at The Shoe. You sure this feeling is true?"

"Oh, praise Jesus. Hurry. Yes, this is true. Please hurry. Hurry. Hurry. I smell it even worse."

Harry sent an unbelieving Sulee home. "What's the

matter with that man? Saturday was always rush day because most of the wives had their husbands' pay and would do their shopping after the dinner meal." Sulee muttered all the way out the door. He flipped the OPEN sign to CLOSED, and picked up the cash box and his newly loaded rifle. His niece had more common sense than any woman should and he believed her eyes. Harry opened the cashbox and dumped the rest of his shot in it. He wrapped the box in his coat, finished buttoning his slicker, put the rifle to his shoulder, and locked the front door. Heading to the church, he figured out how to get Ada out of the charity room without upsetting all the hens. They sure could cackle, and Harry knew better than to get any of that started. If he were to step into the church with his gun, there would be serious trouble. Luckily, there was a dustbin by the rectory. He quietly laid his .22 behind it and headed to the front of the building. He kept the wrapped cashbox under his arm and walked into the narthex and down the hall to the Ladies Guild Room, or as he thought grimly to himself, the Hen House. He knew very few roosters were welcome.

"Good morning, ladies," he greeted from the door. "Could I spare my lovely wife from you for a minute?"

All of the heads whipped around at his voice. Murmurs of response filled the air. The minister was the only male ever in the room, and it was only once a week to get his Saturday noon meal. Harry could feel the inquisitive eyes boring through him. Ada heard him and instinctively sensed something was wrong. She knew Harry hated the Hen House. She put down her sorting, today was stockings and handkerchief day, and walked calmly to him. She said a dictionary of words with her eyebrows, and he answered in kind.

"Darling, I need you at the store. Sulee went home with the grippe."

"I'll get my hat."

Ada shrugged her excuses to the Guild as she gathered her things to make her leave. She knew something bad was happening, but she wasn't about to give the ladies the satisfaction of being the first to know. *Please, sweet Jesus, let it not be family.* She gave Mrs. Gaithers a peck on the cheek, nodded to the others, smiled at Julia and walked to her husband. "Goodbye, my dears, see you tomorrow at services." The couple moved silently down the hall to the front door. It was raining.

"Stay put. Hold this." Harry handed her the coat-wrapped parcel. It was heavy. "I have to fetch something by the rectory. Join me out front as soon as you see me."

"What has happened?" Ada was beginning to shiver.

"Stay put. I'll be right back." He practically sprinted to the dustbin, secured the retrieved rifle under his slicker, and quickly returned. Ada was waiting on the steps, allowing herself to get wet. He stood close to her, hiding what she held. "The cashbox is in my coat. Put it on, but mind the box. I have my gun under my slicker, so I can't help you with it. We have to get to The Shoe."

Her eyebrows reached the sky.

"No, I don't know why. Just hurry."

Ada quickly manipulated the cash and coat. Shrugging it over her shoulders, she kept one arm inside, holding the box. The rain was steady now, and her hat was wilting. Without running to draw attention, they took long strides, free arms linked as though on a stroll. Harry told her about Myra's words and eyes. They loved the girl like no tomorrow and knew she never played a fool with anyone. Their steady stride got them to The Shoe almost before the story was told. Myra and three of the five children were there.

"I sent Junior to fetch Nora Lee. He said she was down to Marjorie's house with her baby dolls."

"Child, what do you want of us?" Aunt Ada took

pride in her ability to organize, be it the church or her family. Myra always knew they were safe when Aunt Ada took charge. She started to quietly weep.

"I smell doom, Aunt Ada. I smell it as sure as I stand here. We have got to go away from here."

"Where, darling?"

"I don't know. Please believe me. We have got to go."

Just then Junior came in without Nora Lee. "That brat won't come home. Why do I have to get her, Mama?"

"Harry, would you go with Junior for the girl." Again the eyebrow dictionary was open in full force. He read the words, spun Junior around and shooed him out the door, steppin' close on his tail.

"I think a picnic upstate would be just the thing. We haven't visited the folks in Texas City in a long while." Ada was aware there wasn't a soul there she knew, but she didn't let on. Texas City was a ferry ride away from Galveston Island, and, while on the Bay, was part of the mainland. "Let's gather some things just in case this rain doesn't stop. We'll tell the children all about the adventure when Junior and Harry get back with Nora Lee. You get the others to pack some clothes. I'll do your food basket, you take care of yourself. Bring blankets for all, you know, for the picnic."

Myra sniffled, breathed deep, and kissed her aunt. She heard every word not spoken. Aunt Ada believed her and was planning to stay away overnight if needed. She ran into her room and got her money. She lined her bosom with the bills and wrapped her coins in a handkerchief, dropping it into one of her apron pockets. Opening her dress, she then took the Canary, blessed it with a kiss and laced it through her stays, securing it against her shimmy. After everything was back in place, she pinned the cameo to her throat. If worse came to worse, she could sell the jewelry. CB's packets of letters were under her mattress, tucked up

170

inside the ticking. Myra dropped them in the pocket besides her coins. "Heavenly Father, keep him safe from whatever this is," she prayed. She got everything off the three beds and the trundle and robbed the blanket safe, taking the winter quilts. She quickly tightened them into bedrolls and bound them with the string she wrapped her sweets.

Aunt Ada was packing the largest basket she could find with all the food she could scrounge up.

"Is there any room in your sweets basket?" she asked.

"'Bout half."

"See what you can do about your jarred peaches."

"Yes, Ma'am." Myra now knew for sure Aunt Ada believed her, because those peaches were a sacred treat. No one in the family was ever allowed to open a jar of peaches until Christmas morning. The fruit would be shared out into everyone's breakfast bowls and then the jar would be passed for each to have a sip of the juice, like so much Communion. Even the babies would get drops on their tongues. Those peaches were the symbol of family. Now Aunt Ada wanted her to pack them in her basket. Maybe she too was starting to smell the fear. Myra packed all six.

Nora Lee banged in the front room, squalling. Junior was hollerin' at her above the racket, and Uncle Harry just stood in the door with his arms folded, water-plastered hair dripping down his collar.

"Missy, you quit your crying, or I'll have your mama give you a reason. Junior, give a hand in the back. The rest of you children, get another set of clothes on over what you have. Don't sass, just do."

Uncle Harry's tone said it all and the brood scattered. Ada came to the front room, her arms full of blankets. Harry nodded to her.

"You and Myra put on another layer of clothes. It's rainin' really hard. Darling, what's your plan?" He knew Ada would know what-was-what.

"We need to get to the ferry line before this rain gets worse. We are taking this fine family on a picnic in Texas City."

Harry's eyes widened. If Ada felt they needed to leave Galveston Island, then this was beyond the notion of smell.

"Do I need to get anything from the house?'

"I need my waterproof. Get yourself your slicker hat and more clothes. You can't button up in Junior's britches. Also." Her eyebrows shot up. "I do think great grandmama's brooch would look fine on this dress I'm wearing."

Great grandmama's brooch was all diamonds and Ada never wore it except on their wedding anniversary. Harry knew she wanted all of her jewels. Great God almighty, this was serious.

"Please hurry, my love. Put the brooch and all in the string pull sachet bag I keep in my glove drawer. I will pack the young'uns and start them toward the ferry. Meet us at the dock. We're going to need tickets. Take care, but hurry." They kissed harder than needed and Harry was gone.

The children were excited. Junior and the twins knew this was no picnic, but the two littlest ones were wanting to take their toys. They'd never been off the island, and the ferry ride was the biggest adventure ever.

Junior just looked at his mother. "We don't take the whole house on a picnic in the rain." He figured out they were in trouble when he saw that the peaches were packed. "I need to know what we are doing."

"We are going to the mainland. I don't know where. I do know why. I smell trouble."

"Mama, is it the dead flowers? I smell it, too." Myra pulled him in for the biggest hug.

"The little ones need not know."

"Yes Ma'am." Off he went, getting them all

outside. Aunt Ada took the house key from Myra, locked the front door and secured the screen. Turning to the children, Ada began to sing.

"We are climbing Jacob's ladder." Theo, quit dragging.

"We are climbing Jacob's ladder." Nora Lee, move faster.

"We are climbing Jacob's ladder." Y'all keep goin'.

"Soldiers of the cross."

Myra took on the song, making up new stanzas. "We are going to the ferry," became a favorite until they saw the crossing ahead. The family came to a dead stop. The dock was packed with so many passengers. It was obvious that others felt the same feeling as Myra. Uncle Harry spotted them all and hurried out of the crowd.

"I got the last eight tickets. The master's a Brother. We need to get aboard." Turning aside to Ada he whispered, "Hurricane. Warning flags are up," and handed her the tickets. He hoisted Nora Lee to his shoulders, took up Theo's bundle, and bull-marched through the crowds, his yellow slicker hat atop Nora Lee. Ada fanned the tickets in front of her bosom, showing all their right to passage. Myra started crying halfway up the gangplank. They were going to be safe.

Chapter 25

MAAMAA

The Tremont House was the finest of the day. All sorts of society functions happened there. This hotel was the center of business deals made and sealed over fine Cuban cigars. Its four story splendor set Young Ike on his heels as he entered the grand lobby with his father. Ike Jameson felt the same. A butler approached them, taking their overcoats and umbrellas. "Suh, it shuh be rainin' cats 'n' dawgs. I'll han' dees to dry. Is that 'ceptable wi' you?"

Ike nodded and took the claim piece. "Son, this is a long way from Brooklyn."

"What, Father?"

"Uh, nothing." His son did not know about Brooklyn, and he sure wasn't going to tell now. "Look at that chandelier. Isn't it something?"

"Oh, yes, Father. Where's dinner going to be?" Young Ike was very excited for the fancy food the banquet promised.

"The invitation says in the fourth floor dining room. Let's head on up."

The lobby led to a wide sweeping staircase that paused at a mezzanine landing. Men were gathered there, looking at a table with name tags and place marks. Young Ike found his father's name right away, but could not find his.

"Father, I can't go in. My name's not there."

Ike looked down at the table and chuckled. "Boy, look at the end of the list." There, after all the men's names was a tag that said Son of Ike Jameson. "Are you my son?"

"Yes sir." With a giant grin, the boy picked up his own marker. They followed the rest of the men to the top floor. The linen, crystal, and china shone in the glow of the newly installed electric lights. 1900 was fine year to be living.

The child held tight to his father's hand. Ike never felt so proud, and was overjoyed to share it with his boy. After introducing the young man to his table mates, they sat down and looked at the menu. The meal was set to start at noon, with speeches at two.

The hotel door-man realized the storm was rising and found his manager, Mr. Brown, who sent him to watch. When the driving rain blocked his view of the street, the man made his report. This time Mr. Brown came to the entrance. He could hear the church bells. He tried to open the giant front doors and could not budge them. Then he knew. He climbed the steps.

While the awards and applause continued, Mr. Brown went from waiter to waiter, telling them to go back into the kitchen as quietly as possible. There he broke the news that a hurricane was soon to hit and the air pressure was keeping the doors closed. In addition to all the traveling guests, the hotel now had seventy some banqueters to care for. All staff was expected to stay and serve.

After the last award was given, Mr. Brown walked swiftly to the front. The crowd was restless from so much sitting, but thought this was part of the program.

"Good afternoon, everyone. My name is Eugene Brown, and I am the general manager of this grand hotel. While you were all enjoying the hospitality of this afternoon there has been a turn in the weather. Our hotel is built so strong, you may not have been aware of the power of the storm outside. However, a hurricane appears to be upon us. The wind is so forceful. The doors refuse to open."

Young Ike looked straight at his father. What was the man talking about? How could doors not open? How would they get home? Was Mother at the church?

"The Tremont House is offering all of you shelter. We will be caring for you until the storm abates. This banquet room will be your home away from home until the doors can be opened again. The staff will be bringing you cots and supper gratis. Standard beverages are waiting. You may start an account at the bar. We offer the finest of premium liquors. Please keep your cigars in the lounge area. Thank you all for staying with us." With a quick turn as to not see anyone who might ask a question, Mr. Brown disappeared into a side office and pulled the call bell for housekeeping.

Cots and bedding quickly arrived. The dining tables were pushed to the side of the room, under the windows. All chairs were set facing out in front of the tables, side by side, making one long velvet bench. There some men sat and watched. Kerosene lamps were filled and stationed around the room, just in case. The cots were lined in rows that allowed clear passage. Each bed was made to exact standards as though the governor himself would be camping on the fourth floor, and not just a group of accountants. However, most of the guests stood in clusters, muttering, complaining, or admiring as was their want, but the uneasiness of their situation could be felt in the room.

The sound of the wind was evident now. It went from moan to shriek to roar. Ike sat on the makeshift bench with his arm around his son. Mr. James Williams, another account manager, sat down beside them with two steaming cups, and smiled.

"I understand our boys know each other." He looked at Ikey. "My boy is James Williams, name same as mine."

Young Ike's eyes opened wide. "James and I are brave friends. You can't call us chicken." He started a giggle. Both fathers laughed at the joke.

"Thank you, sir, for the chicks. That was quite an experience." Ike gave his son a hug.

"That was Mrs. Williams doing, but you are welcome anyway." He offered Ike one of the cups. The men sat in their thoughts, listening. The rain beat on the window behind them. Young Ike sat very still. The wind was screaming "Mama, Maaamaaa". He very quietly mouthed the words of the wind. His father pulled him even closer. Ike softy repeated, "The church is a strong building, Mother is safe, Mother is safe."

Several banqueters were drinking liquor from the bar. The keep dutifully opened accounts for all who asked. It seemed as though this would be a fine afternoon for an excuse to imbibe and enjoy a good smoke. Restaurant staff kept water and coffee on the cleared dais platform. Ike looked around for the privy room. This would be needed quite soon, the way things were going. He'd enjoyed lemonade and coffee with his meal. Young Ike drank so much lemonade his father was wondering if the boy would float away.

"Son, let's find the facilities. They should be through one of those doors." Ike stood, set down his cup, and led his son into the center of the room. He approached one of the waiters and was directed to the third opening along the back wall. The Tremont had indoor plumbing, the first ever installed in the city, and neither Jameson'd ever seen anything like it. Many newly built homes in the finer section of town contained the 'bath room', and Julia had been talking about getting one built in their house. Ike had no idea where in their bungalow it would go, and suggested she think about something else. Now, as he stood next to his son, relieving himself and then allowing his son to pull both chains, he thought maybe he should take another look at their privy closet. This was a wonder that could maybe work, if it didn't cost too much.

Young Ike looked up at his father and smiled. "Mother would like this, don't you think?"

"Yes son, she would. I have been th…"

The world exploded. The sound was not "Mama" any more. The sound was "Shatter, crash, scream". The two buttoned their flies and ran into the main hall just as the largest window hit the tables, sending long jagged shards out to the chairs backed against them. The two spaces, recently vacated for the necessary trip, were covered with glass. Mr. Williams sat cup in hand staring straight ahead, with a triangle of glass embedded deep in the side of his neck. His suit jacket had gone from brown to maroon. Ike started to turn his son from the sight, but not in time. Young Ike was looking at his very first dead man, his friend's father. He vomited right there on the banquet hall carpet. No one said a thing. Two waiters removed the coffee and picked up the dead man, shard intact. They laid him on a table and covered him with a cloth, his blood dripping to the floor. Two more waiters were summoned and the bier was carried into the back room like so many dishes. A maid did the best she could with the vomit and the blood.

Others had small splinters in their hair and hands. Their fellows went quickly to the task of cleaning glass out of each other and housekeepers began to sweep. The wind and rain through the broken window began to shake the other panes. The crowd moved to the cots, watching. The staff worked as though a dead man, flying glass, and terrified patrons were all in a day's assignment. Young Ike pulled himself into a roly-poly bug, all curled on his cot. He hugged his knees to his chest with his head on his father's lap. The tears fell slowly, silently down his cheek. Ike soothed him with handkerchief pats and forehead smoothing. Ikey wasn't brave anymore.

The main door to the banquet hall was closed when the feast started. The entire atmosphere changed when cloth covered serving trolleys entered filled with sandwiches and fresh lemonade. The parade of supper was brought to the outer row of cots. Mr. Brown stood at the door.

"Gentlemen, please make welcome the rest of the guests of this fine hotel. The windows of many rooms are gone. The fourth floor is now the safest location for all."

Those from the banquet, already crowded into the center of the room, stared at the man. There appeared to be hundreds of people behind him. Ladies in fine hats, children in knickers and pinafores, men in suits all stood as though they were ready for seven-course dining. Mr. Brown did not prepare the guests of the lower floors for what they saw. The dining hall was filled with its original refugees. The great window was gone. There were blood stains on the floor. Rain was blowing through the open pane, soaking the patrons and the furniture still close by. Their welcome was not felt.

One hotel guest, a Mrs. Beckham, stopped dead in the entry, gesturing to the room interior. She had three children and what might have been a husband with her. The manager stepped forward in an attempt to open the way.

"My dear sir, what do you propose to do about those people?" Her expansive bosom was draped with more pearls than most jewelry shops carried, and more than one peacock had donated tail feathers to her hat and fan. "My family cannot be expected to be dining in there with those people. It is obvious those people are not of our standing. Return us to our rooms immediately." Her family stayed behind her, watching.

Mr. Brown took a breath and calmly straightened his shoulders. "Madam, you do realize we are in a hurricane, don't you?"

"Of course, you fool. What does that have to do with us?"

"Your rooms are destroyed."

She stared at him. "You will dispatch a maid to retrieve our luggage and refund our payment this very minute, do you understand me?"

"Madam, we will discuss all of this later. Please

step forward so the others behind you can safely enter." Mr. Brown took one of the Beckham children's hands and walked him past his mother. "Come, my young man. Let's show your family to their new accommodations." The Beckhams were lead to a section of cots in the center of the room.

"Madam, I have given you the safest location in the room. Please accept all the hospitality we have to offer." The manager nodded and turned away. Mr. Brown walked back to the entry, the slightest glint smiling in his eyes. The rest of the hotel guests poured into the room. He repeated the announcement about refreshments, liquor and cigars.

Grudgingly, banqueters rose to allow the women to sit on the cots. No one was going near the chair-benches by the tables. The waiters, still in white gloves, were ordered to clean off the broken glass and bring the seats to the cots, allowing husbands to sit with their families. The original honorees were shifted into second-class status in deference to the paying guests. Most were standing since being instructed to relinquish their cots. They soon realized there would be no place for them to rest. The electric lights blinked.

Ike did not move from his ball of a son, and the new guests assumed they were a paying family. Several women murmured over the frightened boy, hush-hushing and petting at him as he lay on his cot. Nodding to the ladies, Ike excused himself and brought back two roast beef sandwiches and more lemonade. He made it to his son's cot just in time. The electric lights blinked, sputtered and stopped shining, leaving the room in grayness. Several women screamed at the dark. Young Ike sat straight up.

"Mother, Mother, where are you? I hear you."

Children were crying, holding on to their parents' arms, legs, or whatever they could grab. Ike put down the roast beef and drinks. He sat on the cot, gathering his son close. He curled him on his lap and rocked him. "The church is strong. Mother is safe. Mother is safe." The sandwiches were forgotten as families found and clung together to fight off the darkening fear and that continuing shriek of wind. Suddenly the electric bulbs flashed bright. A loud "Aaahhh" spread through the room as the families saw their loved ones' faces. Then all of the globes exploded, sending a glitter of glass over everyone. Those wearing hats were protected, but most of the children had taken theirs off, leaving heads and faces exposed. Ike's rocking protected his son, but the sight of blood pouring from those other children brought him to the brink. *Dear God, save my son.*

"Fire!"

Blue flame was sparking from each electrical fixture. The entire room was glowing in what could only be described as the lights of Hell. The wind swayed the chandeliers like so many censers spreading the blessing of Satan over the masses. The wall sconces glowed from the fire they produced. Those standing in the center of the room ran back to the edges where the tables had been stored after the banquet. The windows behind them shook in the wind. With no chandelier directly overhead, the Ikes stayed on the cot, watching the panic in fear.

"Ho-shi-e-ni, naf-shi, OAdonai. Ho-shi-e-ni, naf-shi, OAdonai". Ike was praying the only prayer he remembered from him childhood.

"What kind of talk is that, Father?" Young Ike sat himself up, pushed away from his father and looked at him. This was gibberish, and his father never even spoke baby loving to him when he was little. Had the Devil himself entered his father? "Are you possessed?"

"Oh, my son, no, I am praying. It means 'Save me, my soul, oh Lord.' It is the true tongue of Jesus, Hebrew." Ike had not spoken his childhood prayer since Brooklyn, and shocked himself at the remembering. "I said this prayer when I was little."

The wind shifted, pounding rain against the remaining window panes. Branches, shingles, and startled birds were crashing against them. The water poured through the hole where the great window shattered, carrying the stunned birds and debris. The swinging lamps seemed to have run out of fuel and were dancing macabre. The people fell silent, waiting for the end of the world.

"The Lord is my shepherd, I shall not want." A small girl's voice trembled but continued. Her father joined in the words. "He maketh me to lie down in green pastures, He restoreth my soul." Bit by bit the refugees joined the Psalm. Mothers held their children, fathers held their families, and the original occupants of the room linked arms with each other, with colored butlers, with waiters, with housekeepers. They all knew they were doomed.

The night was spent in terror. The glow of the oil lamps lit by Mr. Brown, offered small comfort. The rest of the glass blew sometime during the late evening. The rain poured in, soaking the floor. The cot blankets did little to tent the children. Mr. Brown organized a linen brigade, having staff stripping each room below for sheets, blankets, and towels to dry the floor. The banqueters and male guests alike worked at sopping the mess. Once each cloth was saturated, staff returned the linens to the second and third floors. The flood water had risen pass the first landing and was lapping at the mezzanine. The children were herded to the center cots and the women took turns between holding the oil lamps for the men and tending to the young ones. This helped abate the crying, as the children could see the work being done.

"My papa's saving me," said a little girl with a crusted gouge in her cheek.

"So is mine. Look, there he is now." Her cot mate snuggled beside her. Children of lamp holders were doubled with those whose parents were close by. Not once throughout the night did a cry go unanswered.

Young Ike was sitting with a boy a few years younger and he took it upon himself to be the child's strength. This task made his fear fade in the background. As he hugged the child, he daydreamed. *Mother would be so proud of them when they got home. Maybe she would continue to be kind to Father once she knew how hard he'd worked at keeping the room dry. Maybe they could get running water and plumbing, too.* Those thoughts set him to thinking about how nice she kept things. *Mother always worked so hard to clean the house and the church. Hopefully the beautiful stained glass windows in the sanctuary wouldn't get too dirty in the storm.* Eventually both boys slept.

"Sir, excuse me."

Ike looked up to see that he was handing wet linens to a familiar face. He recognized the red headed fishman's girl.

"Yes? Oh, I know you. My office is at the wharves. I see you with the fishman. Isn't your name Margurite? Why are you here?"

"I help serve with my Mamam when they have banquets. Usually though, I'm with the cook. Sir, please hand me your bundle. I'll take it away."

It was past midnight. "Listen. Listen. The wind is changing." One of Mr. Brown's task was directing the water removal. The workers and what children were awake fell silent. Where once there was a scream there was now a moan bordering on a sigh. The rain become a minor torrent and was falling straight down.

"Fellow guests, please take a break. There are still sandwiches on the trays. I will bring in cake." Where Mr. Eugene Brown conjured up cake will always be a mystery, but there it was. While everyone was working the linens, he'd brewed strong coffee on the coal stove in the service area. Long abandoned for the convenience of electricity, it sat empty, being used for storage. Mr. Brown broke up several chifferobes for fuel, dutifully recording their source and use. All were served, including the maids and butlers who assisted him. Mothers carried their lamps from cake to cots and some of the sleepers woke to the oddest party they'd ever seen. The wind continued to wane.

At first light Mr. Brown went down the back stairway. The water was gone but the passage between first and second was filled with trash and not a few dead rats. He retreated to the fourth and tried the front steps. The expanse of this stairway kept the large pieces of floating wood from completely blocking the way. The grand entry doors were intact, but he had a very hard time pushing them. When he finally got them open, he stared. A woman in a mud-stained blue dress lay drowned outside the door, a mule carcass on top of her.

Chapter 26

HUMMINGBIRD CAKE AND MULES

The buzz of gossip rose in the Guild Room after Ada left. All the women knew the rules. You may speak about another member, but only with kindness. It was the twist of those words that told the truth.

"I hope poor Miss Sulee recovers quickly." *Hmm, is she in a family way? It is the morning, you know.*

"Mr. Harry seemed really in need of Ada's help." *Everyone knows they quibble in the store. That's why she came to the Guild. Hmmmm.*

"We should stop by on Monday and make sure the girl is well." *To check to see if she is showing. Um,mmmmmmm.*

The ladies finally settled into the rhythm of sorting. Stocking Saturday brought out extra help, women with the gift of fine stitchery. Silk threads were used to darn the stockings, and this art seemed to be dying. Of course the young wives could mend their men's cotton socks, but few could work the silks so the hosiery looked brand new. Mrs. Gaithers always brought her sisters on those days. Unlike the wooden darning eggs of most households, these sisters used exquisitely painted porcelain ones. Their grandmother emigrated from Europe, bringing with her the ability to pull the silk to just the right tautness. She passed the art to all the mothers and daughters in the family. These women made stocking day at the church their chance to visit without their husbands around. They always packed a dinner hamper and didn't go home until after the noon meal. The Ladies Guild Room became a hen house of rooster rumpling whenever the sisters brought their darning eggs.

"My Walter is driving me mad with his thoughtlessness. If I have told him once, I have told him dozens of time to remove his boots before he tramps in from the back. He walks dirt straight through to the kitchen where he sits in his chair to take them off. When I point out the trail, he just asks me when am I going to put his chair on the back stoop. I tell him furniture is for inside not outside and to sit on the steps to take them off. He says steps are for feet, not bottoms."

Several ladies smiled at this. Mrs. Wallace, Mrs. Gaithers middle sister, told this same story every time. Gray was showing through her rich black hair. Some of the hens wondered if the streaks were caused by her stubbornness. Lord knew why she wouldn't have a stoop bench built like everyone else does. Julia mentioned it to her one time and learned quickly. Mrs. Wallace does not take suggestion well.

"Child, you must not understand my circumstances, or you would not make such a comment."

The room hummed at that one. It was well known that the Wallaces squeezed two pennies together to make three and were quite able to buy the lumber for the bench. Whatever 'circumstances' affected Mrs. Wallace were of her own making, and the Guild knew from then on to let her ramble on uninterrupted, bless her heart.

The third sister, Miss Annie, had not earned her Mrs. Miss Annie Hoffen was the eldest of the girls and showed it with her dominance. She worked the finest stitch and spoke the sharpest tongue. However, the chiding was reserved for her sisters, and everyone else enjoyed her company. The Guild knew she sacrificed her youth to raise her siblings and care for their mother after Father died fighting the Indians in '79. They did not know about the secret hanging on her cross chain.

"Ladies, I am so thrilled to be with you." Annie seemed extra jittery this stocking day. Justine noticed Annie was tangling her silks, and that never happened. "I love getting out of the house and listening to all of you talk about your men. They certainly are a wonder." Thoughts of Carl were bubbling close to the surface. Too close. A three year secret is hard to keep.

The ladies decided to open their baskets. Stocking Saturday was special in many ways. Each time they met for this chore, they packed their dinners. The women knew the others would be noticing the different meals, and this event became an unspoken competition of the kitchens of the Methodist community. Each woman brought enough to share.

"Oh my, Annie, I see you brought your hummingbird cake. You have such a large piece. May I have a taste?" Annie's 'piece' was half a cake and all the women stepped over to admire.

"Of course. I hope you like it. I've been told it is delicious. 'Best in the world' he, uh, she said." No one noticed her blunder. *I have got to shut my mouth*, she thought to herself.

"If I was a betting woman, and I am not, I would wager this to be the finest luncheon on the whole island." Mrs. Nicholson, the Reverend's wife, was a betting woman. Her bid Whist could be cut-throat. She smiled, "Who wants to bet we will see my husband in this room in the next few minutes?" Reverend Nicholson knew when his dear Linda Sue packed a dinner basket for Guild. On Stocking Saturday he would just have to leave his study and visit. Oh my, those women could put out a delicious spread.

All the women laughed. "Linda Sue, you must be able to see the future." More laughter.

"I think we all can." Mrs. Nicholson set out the extra plate she always brought. That man of hers could be counted on to show up as soon as the church bells started.

Church bells were rung, chiming the hour, and many households danced to the sounding of the bells, breakfast between six and eight, dinner at twelve, and supper any time after six. The ladies took out their many offerings and arranged them on the sideboard. Noon bell meant singing the Doxology and fine eating. They waited.

The sounding began. The women circled and held hands. The eleventh chime meant Ada would use her pitch pipe set to F major, the starting note, but Ada was gone to the store, who knows why. Julia took the lead and hummed as close to F as she could get. Twelve chimes. "Praise God from..." Another chime and then another. The women sang above the bells, looking toward the ceiling in the direction of the tower. The bell boy must have gone mad. They turned to the sideboard, filling their plates, and sitting at their places wondering why that young man would keep ringing past twelve.

Reverend Nicholson crashed open the door and ran in as fast as his round body would let him.

Linda Sue smiled. "Hello, darling, here is your plate. We hoped you could join us." He stared at his wife and all of the hens. They were sitting, eating and chatting as though it were yesterday.

"My God, Linda Sue, don't you hear the bells?"

"Of course. Has the poor boy gone insane? Please put some dinner on your plate."

"Linda Sue, we are in a hurricane. Look at your floor."

Miss Annie rushed to the door. "Dear God in Heaven, Mother," The narthex and the hall leading to the Guild room were becoming a river of filth. "Oh, Mother." Annie froze, and started to scream. Their house was far downhill from the church. The sisters realized the meaning of the horror and joined Annie in her panic. "Mother, Mother, Mother. Oh my Jesus, Mother." Annie could not walk, could not catch her breath. She reached for her cross, pulling it out of her bodice. Right there in the middle of the panic she opened the clasp and put her engagement ring on her left hand, dropping the rest of the jewelry in her pocket. *I will die an engaged woman*, she thought. *I love you, Carl.*

"Move ladies, now. The choir room is high enough. Fill your baskets and let's go. Jesus loves us, but we must help ourselves." Linda Sue gathered up Annie and dragged her toward the steps, the sisters following, all in shock. The women scrambled to collect the food and their belongings. Quickly, they all trailed the Reverend through the water to the loft steps. Several were starting to push to get in the passage. All were weeping. Julia, in the middle of the crowd, stopped stock still. Her son and husband were up hill from the church. She would go there.

"For God's sake, Julia, move. What is that matter with you? Can't you see the floor is almost covered? Move, child, move." Justine was last in line, as was her place, and surprised herself at her forcefulness.

"I am going to the Tremont. My men are there. Ike is receiving an award. It will be just as safe as the choir room." With a deaf ear to the protestors, Julia walked through the water in the hall and out the door to the steps. No one suspected what Julia knew. Her monthly was weeks late. She was expecting. She had to go to her family.

Her new clothes were soaked at the hem. Down one step and her skirt was ruined. She pulled it up and stepped down into a river. As fast as possible she headed up the hill. The wind was crying. She was drenched to the skin. "I will do this. Oh, Mama, I will do this." The water was up to her knees and she hiked her skirt higher. She could see the hotel. "Oh, my darlings, oh my child, I'm coming."

The water was vile. Floating branches and dead animals were everywhere. "Oh, Ike, keep our baby safe. I love you both." Her climbing was keeping pace with the flooding. The soaked fabric of her beautiful periwinkle outfit was slowing her. She had one block to go. The water was up past her knees. Unspeakable filth was all around. A floating branch knocked her dinner basket from her arm. Julia stopped and stood, stupidly watching it swirl out of reach. The hope of feeding her son in the storm was gone, sunk in the mire. The sobs began. When the rise of the water reached mid-thigh, she gathered her skirt, lifting it almost as high as her waist and pushed on. She never saw the mule.

Chapter 27

HEADLINES AND HEARTACHE

FIVE THOUSAND LIVES BLOTTED OUT

Galveston Horror Proves More Terrible Than First Reported.

Over Two Thousand Bodies Already Recovered.

Ghoulish Acts of Vandalism-The Dead Buried at Sea.

Los Angeles Times Sept.12, 1900

Ike never saw the headlines. No one did. Mayor Jones was finally able to send telegraphs appealing for help on September 11, a date far too late. No mayor could give him back his wife, his house, his docks. All was lost.

Mr. Brown opened the back loading area, allowing the hotel survivors their exit. Holding hands, Ikey, his father, and some of the other refugees stepped out into the receding water. Those getting their bearings bid farewell to their new friends and left, walking around the walls of the Tremont into the remnants of Hell. The Ikes did not move. The boy started to sob.

"Mother. Find Mother."

"Oh, Son. Yes. Now." Neither could speak coherently. "Church. Safe." Ike took a deep breath and began walking down the back alley of the hotel, away from Tremont Avenue. At the end of the lane he turned the corner toward the bay, knowing the church would be in sight. What they saw was nothing, nothing they could recognize. All the houses, all the shops, all the stables were gone. No trees, no lawns, no streets. They stood shocked, looking at broken timbers as far as the eye could see. That, and something no small boy, or man for that matter, should ever witness. Death. Bodies of people and animals were everywhere. The human bodies and animal carcasses sprawled up, over, and around the debris, mixed together as though all had been playing ring-a-rosy, all fall down. Both Ikes froze.

"Mother. Church. Now." The son pulled on the father's hand. "Mother. Church. Now. Look for the steeple." Ikey jerked his father's arm hard, bringing him back from his shock. "You're tall. Look for the steeple."

"Yes, son." Ike slowly began breathing, pushing his panic down. He raised his eyes to the heavens, silently praying for strength, strength for today. Then he looked to the horizon and saw the steeple. *Oh, thank you God, the building stands.* "Yes, son, look where I'm pointing. You're right. I see the steeple."

The two started walking, keeping the spire in sight. There was no passageway. They climbed over the timbers, around the carcasses when they could, and on them when they couldn't. Other survivors were with them, but they took no notice. All they saw was the steeple. It took more than two hours to travel the short distance to the church.

The great doors were gone. Ikey started shouting at the front steps. His "Mother, Mother" echoed in the filth-filled narthex. There was no response. "Halloo", called Ike. "Is anyone here? Julia, Julia Jameson, where are you?" Nothing. "Reverend Nicholson, Missus Linda Sue, anyone here?" Dead silence. "Juullia." The echoes answered.

They stumbled their way into the sanctuary. "Halloo. Halloo. Is anyone here?"

"Up here. Up here in the choir loft. Who goes there?" A familiar voice called back.

"Reverend Nicholson. Oh thank God. Are you well?

Is Missus Linda Sue with you? This is Ike Jameson." Father and son started toward the altar. Pews were everywhere, upside down or on their sides, hymnal racks scattering their contents. "Is everyone safe? Where is my wife?"

"Linda Sue and I are safe. We all sheltered in the choir room. Everyone survived and went on to their families. We're coming. Just wait. " The Nicholson's made their way down the loft steps the best they could. The Ikes were greeted with much affections and blessings.

"What do you mean, 'where is my wife?' She's with you." Reverend Nicholson was puzzled.

Ike looked at the Reverend and his wife. "No. We haven't seen her. She came here for Saturday stocking day."

Linda Sue spoke up. "Yes, but she left when the storm hit. Said you were at the Tremont and that she would find you all there. You mean to tell us that she's not with you. Oh, dear Jesus. Where could she be?" The silence between them was unbearable.

"Mother." The boy fell into Mrs. Nicholson's arms where he was pulled fiercely into her bosom. They all sank onto the chancel steps as reality hit. Julia was gone, out there, somewhere. Ike began to sob along with his boy.

"Son," the Reverend began after getting the nod from his wife. "Son, leave your child with us. We are going to be staying in the choir room. The rectory is gone. Linda Sue and I will watch him while you look for Julia."

"No, Father." Ikey looked up from Mrs. Nicholson's arms. "No, Father, let me come with you. Remember. I'm brave." The adults all noticed that he had not stirred from his bosomy nest.

"Darlin'," cooed Linda Sue Nicholson. "I need your help in straightening up the mess this storm has made of our hymnals. Won't you stay and help us? Your father will be back as soon as he finds your mother."

"Is it alright with you, Father? I could help you find Mother." His voice was muffled.

"The Reverend and Mrs. Nicholson really need your help." He stood up. "I'll be back very soon." He kissed his son on the top of his head and shook the Reverend's hand. "Thank you both. I will find her. By God, I will find her." Ike walked down the aisle and out into utter desolation.

His first goal was to find his house. When he got to where he thought South Lowman Street should be, he found nothing but the same. Destruction and dead animals hid all recognizable signs. He wandered, dazed, until he saw one green shutter sticking out of the rubble. That was the only thing that told him he was home. Many of his neighbors were not so lucky. On top of the splinters was a muddy gray and purple striped dress spread out as though waiting for its wearer. He'd never seen it before and wondered at the power of the storm.

He traveled for two days, looking for his Julia. He was numb to the stench of death. It was horridly hot. He didn't notice. He just kept moving, calling her name, stopping to search each pile of corpses waiting to be buried.

"Mr. Jacobson, Mr. Jacobson. It's me, Mr. Thomas. You know, from the office." A tattered boy was grasping his arm. "Mr. Jacobson, you have to come with me. Now."

Ike stared at him stupidly. "What? Why?"

"I found your wife."

Chapter 28

FAMILY TIES

"Maamaa, Benjy's peein' out the screens again."

"Benjy, use the pot. You know better. Nora Lee, quit tattlin'." Myra Gallaway Ledbetter had it up to there with those children. Blessings from God and all that aside, she had a terrible itch for what was. Back when she was poor, she could turn the young'uns out and walk the docks to sell her sweets. The hurricane changed all that. Now, dammit, she was married, living in a really big house and was somewhat financially secure, knock on wood. Of course, she loved her young'uns and the new one comin', *bless its heart*, but she knew she was never meant to be a housewife. If only Julia was here to teach her how. Myra whispered a quick prayer for her late sister-in-law and crossed herself, even though she wasn't Catholic. Damned mule. Oops, two curses. "Ladies are supposed to watch their language. I don't see that ever happening, lady or language," she muttered to herself as she rested her swollen feet on the low stool in front of her.

"Whhhhhhat, Mama?" Nora Lee was playing with the new dollhouse Uncle Harry built for her. It was just like the one she lived in. There was a parlor, dining room, bathroom, kitchen with side breakfast room down stairs and three bedrooms up. A screened sleeping porch was out over the back stoop. Aunt Ada fixed it up with fancy curtains for the dollies. Not even the sharpest eye could find the fabric missing from inner seams of the big house parlor draperies. Nora Lee arranged all the doll furniture to match her home. One of the boy dolls was at the sleeping porch screens, obviously up to no good. The child had him standing facing out on a tiny chair pushed up to the windows. One could only imagine where she got that idea.

"Darlin', show Benjy where the bathroom is. You

don't want to clean up doll pee-pee, now do you?" Nora Lee giggled and swooped the toy into the toilet room, where the activity was concluded with the girl announcing, "Now flush."

All the dolls were named. Mama and Papa CB were standing outside of the miniature front door, kissing good-bye. Franky and Theo were sitting at the dining room table. Tiny dishes were in front of them, but Nora Lee hadn't decided what to serve. She'd taken bread dough and made doll-sized food for the plates. The girl doll stood beside the table, and you could almost see her tapping her toe impatiently. One chair was conspicuously empty. The Junior brother doll was put away.

"Maamaa, when is Junior coming home? I miss him." Nora Lee left the dolls and climbed up beside her mother on the settee. "I left a kitchen chair empty for him just in case today is the day." She snuggled close to her mother's side and absently hugged the unborn baby. She didn't know much about such things, but she knew her mama's tummy looked 'bout to explode. The baby moved under her arm.

"Darlin', did you feel that? I think it likes you lovin' it." Truth was, Myra had less than a month, but she'd take today, God willin'. *Sure is a lot easier carrying a baby in your arms than in your belly,* she thought. Her feet were killing her.

"When is Junior coming back?" The girl wasn't one to be sidetracked.

"When the new store is finished. Uncle Harry and Aunt Ada need him to help the workmen with the fetching and the hammering more than we need him here." Myra was proud her oldest was that kind of child, always wanting to pitch in. When the hurricane took the Masonic Temple, it took the store, too. Ada and Harry lost everything, including the house. The Shoe was knocked over on its side and all their things were washed away. Thank you, Sweet

Jesus, for the smell of doom that saved them all. Myra couldn't ever imagine life without her family. How CB found them, housed with all the other refugees, she'll never know, however he did, and what he said next knocked them all flat.

***

Myra, the children, Aunt Ada and Uncle Harry were staying at the local Catholic church in Texas City. The priest, Father Ed, said all were welcome and you didn't have to attend daily Mass, but would you please clear off the pews you were sleeping on so that rightful worshipers could sit. They all agreed it was a very small price to pay. Sometimes the women would sit in the back, just to hear the sing-song of the Latin. Being a good Mason, Harry never stepped foot into their temporary abode during all that 'bell ringin, smoke shakin' voodoo'. He made sure the children did not see the 'mackerel snappers' doing whatever they did. He'd never been to a Mass in his life, but if the Catholics didn't approve of the Masons, he didn't approve of them. Myra and Aunt Ada agreed to not tell Harry they kind-of liked all the goin's on. The sound of the prayers was soothing and the incense smelled like hope.

Myra's warning and the preparation for flight was serving them well. When they got off the ferry at Texas City the storm was starting its horrible destruction of Galveston Island. Yes, they were being blown and soaked, but the Island took the force. The local Constabulary assigned a deputy to the dock and guided all with no place to stay to the churches in town. Harry was far too wet to refuse St. Mary's hospitality, but just knew his Brothers would not approve. He did not realize until later that the Temple was gone, as were many of the unmarried members who went there for safety, feeling the flood would never reach the building's second story. This horrible news would come later.

The family brought food, blankets and clothing. The

priest showed them to their places in the pews and Ada quickly organized them into their own little nest. There they stayed for several weeks, not touching the peaches. The Knights of Columbus and their wives provided morning coffee, a cup of milk for each child, biscuits with butter, jam, and slab bacon slices. The Oblates of Mary served a filling supper in the late afternoon, leaving extras for the mothers to feed their children again before bedtime.

One day, as Ada and Myra were tidying their spot, they heard a holler from the back of the church.

"MYYYYYYRA, Myra Gallaway, are you there?"

Heads whipped at the sound. Myra stood stock still. She knew that voice. CB, her CB was here. She turned, scooted her way down the row of pews to the center aisle, and ran crying, smack dab into her man. Tipped off balance, they landed on the floor and exchanged their first kiss. It was wonderfully long.

"Oh thank God, oh thank God, oh thank God you're alive." They were saying the same words to each other, shaking and sobbing, petting at each other. All the commotion around them disappeared as they held tight for what seemed like an eternity.

"Ahem, Niece. Who it this man you are rolling down the aisle with?" Uncle Harry was towering over the two kissing on the marble floor. Looking straight up at Harry, CB went bright red, what with his blond hair and fair, but tanned complexion. Not letting loose of Myra, he spoke.

"I am CB Ledbetter and I love this woman."

"That's just dandy. May I suggest you help her into an upright position? The floor of the center aisle of St. Mary's Catholic Church is not the proper place to court my niece." He extended his hand. "I'm Harry Dickenson, and I love this woman, too." The shake led to a lift and CB was on his feet, pulling Myra with him. Harry turned to her.

"Why haven't you brought this fine young man

'round to dinner?" Harry had that 'what's the story, young lady' look. "Your Auntie would have told me if you had a beau."

Myra demurred. "Uncle Harry, this is CB Ledbetter. CB, please meet my beloved uncle, Harry Dickenson. CB became my beau, you are my beau, aren't you, right before the hurricane. He is Julia Jacobson's brother." Her eyes went from sparkle to clouds.

"Yes sir, I am her beau. I told her I loved her. She didn't get a chance to say it back." He looked around. "Is Flossie and the Ikes with you? Where are your children? I can't wait to see everyone."

"The children are somewhere around and about the church. Aunt Ada is over there, sweeping where we sleep. I heard that Little Ike and his daddy survived the storm by staying in the Tremont." She fell dead silent.

"Where is Flossie?"

Myra's eyes said it all before the words came. She led him to the closest pew. Sitting, holding his hands, she told him everything she knew.

"They found her drowned under a mule at the Tremont door. No one there knew she was the wife and mother of two of the refugees on the fourth floor. Her body was unidentified and loaded with the others on a wagon for one of the grave ships." Myra was shaking. "Oh CB, luckily she ended on top of the pile. One of the counting men passing by recognized her." Myra was sobbing. "Ike was brought to the wagon and claimed her. She was given a ground burial, thank God. The counting man was here the other day and told me all about it. That's how I know. He had seen us together on the docks and though I should know the story. Oh, my darling, did you hear what happened with the grave ships?"

CB was pasty white, staring at Myra. "No."

Myra looked at Uncle Harry. He took up the story. "The boats went out in the water to bury the dead. Many of those poor souls were washed back on shore. The conditions there were beyond belief, so we were told. I am forever grateful my family was safe and did not see those hideous corpses." He shook his head as though to dispel the stories of the waterlogged, bloated bodies floating in the surf and splitting open on the sand under the hot sun, their putrid entrails for all to see.

"The man told me that Ike and Ikey are staying with Brother Rabbi Cohen and his wife until they get back on their feet," Uncle Harry continued. "Seems like Ike and Esther Cohen knew each other from way back. Rabbi Cohen is a good man, a fine Mason. Your family will be well cared for."

Myra turned to her sweetheart, pulled him close, and rocked him like one of her babies. CB wept until he could not. Then he pulled away, rubbing his cheek. He looked her straight in the eye.

"What was that?"

"My bosom." Sniffling, it was her turn to blush.

"Beside that. What made the dent in my cheek?"

"Your ring. I call it The Canary because it's yellow. I keep it tied to my stays."

"Can you untie your stays?"

"Here in a church? You are not going to make love to me right here, are you?"

CB was red all over again. "No. I just want the ring."

Myra's eyes went wide. "What? You nasty rotten skunk, so that's why you found me. Well, dammit, you can have your ring back." She turned her back and fumbled with her blouse and shimmy. A few seconds later, ring loosed and in her hand, she turned back to face that low down ship rat. He was on one knee, right there in the church aisle, looking in her eyes.

"Myra Gallaway, would you marry me?"

"Huh?"

"I repeat. Myra Gallaway, would you marry me? If you say yes, I will put that ring where it belongs, on your left hand."

She handed him the ring and held out her right hand, still wearing her wedding band on her left. "Where do you suppose we will live? My children can't sleep in ship hammocks." She then looked at Uncle Harry, who was watching patiently as all unfolded. "He's a sailor," she said to him, as though that explained everything.

"Son, we need to introduce you to my wife, and we need to have a talk. Myra's right, you cannot keep her and the family on a boat."

"Sir, I own a fine house upstate. It has a bathroom," he added with pride. Niece and Uncle stared dumbfounded. Myra started crying all over again.

**

Within the week, Myra and CB were married by the priest, who forgave them their Protestantism, figuring wedlock in was better than wedlock out. What really shocked Father Ed was the fact that the groom had colored standing right up there next to him as best man.

"He's not a legal witness," Father protested. CB insisted that the signature of *Jack Smith* rest directly below *Harry Dickenson*.

"What do you mean, he's not legal?" CB gave the priest the best 'Mama' look he could muster up. "This man is my brother." Father Ed did not say another word until he began the ceremony. The family joyfully opened jars of peaches for the reception.

Everyone settled into the house in LaPorte. With the docks destroyed, CB was able to be at home, learning how to be a husband and daddy. The daddy part came easy, the husband part was all new to him and took practice. He liked practicing. Aunt and Uncle had several weeks before the land where their house stood would be ready to build a new store. No more leasing for them. The Masons decided to build with stone so the rage of Poseidon would never destroy their Temple again. The Dickensons would stay with the Ledbetters until the upstairs living quarters were finished and furnished. Then the store below could be completed and stocked. Ada decided it must have plumbing upstairs and down. She couldn't stop admiring all those pipes and porcelain in the LaPointe house.

One day Aunt Ada went to buy eggs, milk and wash soda from the local merchant. She always liked to run the errands, going to a different shop each time, getting ideas for their own mercantile. However this time she practically ran home.

"Harry, Myra, guess who I just talked to?" She was panting so heavily she had to sit down.

"Beelzebub?" Harry answered.

"Who, Aunty, who?" Myra gave her uncle a scowl and brought a glass of water from the faucet.

"Miss Annie from church." Ada was smiling, sipping the water. "She isn't Miss Annie."

Harry cricked his left eyebrow at her. "Tarnation woman, if Miss Annie isn't Miss Annie, who is she?"

Ada looked at everyone and announced, "Miss Annie is Mrs. Carlton Wilson. She's married and lives right here in LaPorte."

"Good Lord, is her husband the Carlton Wilson who was the business partner of her daddy, Otto? He must be one hundred and two years old." Uncle Harry couldn't imagine anyone getting married at that age.

Ada smiled. "Darling, you are older than either of them," and ruffled her husband's silver hair. She turned to Myra, giving her a nudge. "Seems they had been secretly courting just like somebody else I know. They got married just as soon as they buried her mother, God rest her soul. Her husband has a very nice house here, just like you do, and her sisters and brothers-in-law are living with them."

"Humph," said Harry, smoothing his mane. "That's

certainly a strange turn of events, her supporting them. I wonder how long that'll last."

"Now, Husband, mind your tongue." Ada swept her eyes around the room she was sitting in.

"Silly Auntie." Myra put her arms around Ada. "You know this is your house, too." With a smooch for both, Myra went upstairs to check on the children. They'd been quiet way too long.

Time passed, and soon enough Jack was sent to fetch CB back to sea. As the couple kissed goodbye at the door, Myra whispered in her husband's ear.

"Are you sure?"

"Yes, darling, I'm sure."

His Rebel yell was probably heard all the way to the Island.

"I promise you I will be everything my daddy wasn't."

"You already are. Mister CB Ledbetter, I love you."

With another hug, he was gone. Turning back to the house, she smiled. "Guess I better tell them all why he was hollering." Touching her flat front, she spoke. "Oh, baby child, you are loved. You are wanted. Just wait until you get here. However, don't let your sister Nora Lee see you misbehave. She is one big ol' tattle tale." Myra raised her left hand to her lips and kissed the Canary. She closed her eyes and made a wish. Smoothing her skirt, she walked in the front door, knowing all was right with this world, at least for today.

THE END

About the Author:

Some people call Jacqueline Moore a snowbird because she spends so much time writing in South Carolina. Not so. She loves the Ohio winters with all the ice and snow. She says, "Traveling south in the summer makes me a sunflower...and a beach bum!" As a writer and educator, Jacqueline surrounds herself with words. She savors the sounds and sense of letters put together to create a lasting memory. Her debut novel, THE CANARY, is inspired by a most beautiful yellow diamond that rests on her finger and the whispered family secrets about how it got there.

Please visit her at www.jacqueline-t-moore.com and on Facebook at Jacqueline T. Moore for conversations and updates on her next book.

Acknowledgements:

With deepest heartfelt love, I hug my daughter, Julie Anne Jacobs. She is my reader, listener, hand-holder, and most of all, my tow truck when I get stuck in the mud. Thank you, Martha Moody, for your book inscription that inspired me more than you will ever know. Thank you, Katrina Kittle, for providing my Christmas present. Many thanks go out to George James and Pat Reinhart for their guidance and reading. I give a special thank you to my colloquialism coach who is fine as frog's hair. Thank you, Sherry Derr-Wille, my editor. You taught me more about writing than I ever learned before. I sincerely appreciate the lessons.

<u>Social Media Links:</u>

Facebook: https://www.facebook.com/pages/Jacqueline-T-Moore/476568419146045

Website: www.jacqueline-t-moore.com

Email: Jacqueline@jacqueline-t-moore.com

Myra sells cookies to survive, delicious sounding cookies. Below are the recipes for these treats!

JUMBLES

Adapted from Eliza Leslie's 1857 cookbook

Jumbles
Makes about 3 dozen
1 cup lard, softened
1 cup sugar
1 egg
1 tablespoon rose water (use ¾ teaspoon vanilla)
3 cups sifted flour
½ teaspoon salt
½ teaspoon baking soda
1/2 teaspoon cinnamon
¾ cup raisins
¾ cup large semisweet chocolate chunks
1/2 cup chopped pecans
1/2 cup sliced almonds
additional sugar

Preheat Oven to 375 degrees F. Sift flour with spices. Set aside. Cream lard and sugar until very light. Add egg and rose water, blending thoroughly, Add dry ingredients all at once to creamed mixture, blending well. Drop by teaspoon on ungreased cookie sheets. Bake 10-12 minutes or until lightly browned around edges. Remove to a rack, sprinkle with sugar, and cool.

(note)   Myra used lard because she couldn't afford butter. Butter is better.

PLUNKETS

Adapted from Janet McKenzie Hill's 1902 cookbook
Practical Cooking and Serving; A Complete Manual of
How to Select, Prepare, and Serve Food

Plunkets
1 cup lard
½ cup flour
1 cup sugar
¾ cup cornstarch
6 eggs
2 teaspoons baking powder
1 teaspoon vanilla
Cream lard, add sugar, beating until foamy. Separate eggs. Beat whites until dry. Beat yolks until thick. Pour yolks over whites and gently fold together. Sift, twice, flour, cornstarch, baking powder. Slowly add eggs to creamed lard mixture. Then add dry ingredients and vanilla. Bake in individual greased tins. Ice or not as desired.
(note) Bake time and temperature were not recorded. I am suggesting 350 degrees for 10 minutes and then check. Please remember, butter is better.

CRYBABIES
Adapted from a collection of recipes from the 1800's submitted by Frances Lindsey and Helen Gravell. to <u>Heritage Cook Book.</u> (author unknown)

Crybabies
½ cup lard
½ cup brown or white sugar
½ cup molasses
½ cup raisins
½ cup chopped pecans
1 teaspoon baking soda
½ cup strong hot coffee
½ teaspoon ginger
½ to 1 teaspoon cinnamon
¼ teaspoon salt
2 cups flour

Preheat oven between 350-375 degrees
Mix lard, sugar, molasses, raisins and pecans. Disolve soda in the hot coffee and add to batter. Sift dry ingredients and stir into liquid mixture. Drop from spoons onto greased cookie sheets.
Bake 12-15 minutes. Let set up 5 minutes before removing from sheet.

(note) Please remember, butter is better.

BOOK CLUB GUIDELINES:

THE CANARY

Is this book believable? Explain why you liked your favorite scene. Describe the book in one sentence. How would you recommend this book to another person?

Who is your most memorable character and why? What choices/ challenges does the character face? What would you have done differently if you were in their shoes?

Did you notice any symbolism used in the book? Explain.

Do the speech patterns add or detract from the read? Which words or phrases did you enjoy? Were there any you felt concerned or confused about?

If you could go to that Galveston neighborhood in 1899, who would you be? How do you identify with some of personalities/problems of these people from over one hundred years ago?